Grains of Sand

E.H. KANA

Grains of Sand

ISBN: 978-1-7772535-7-8

CONTENTS

AUTHOR''S NOTE

E.H Kana is the pen name, the nom de plume, the nom de guerre of the author, E.H Mutubuki. The experiences, the incidents and characters described though based on real events and people, are all fictitious. So any coincidence in name or character is mere accident and not intended. So noone should take offence at all.

All the same, there is a lot of the author himself in the lively, dynamic and indomitable character of Dumba. For very few people commit their experiences, their memories to paper, or tell them to others. And it is from these that the essence of the horrendous life experiences as well as the joys can be distilled. As the Chinese saying aptly illustrates: a good memory is not as good as a little ink. The hardship is there, and also the heartache, but it can be muted. The overiding theme is one of exhilaration, of opportunities not to be missed, of character tempered in a crucible of adversity. Though as a human being the author, through the main character Dumba, sports inconsistency and contains every possible contradiction, those who find him vain, extravagant, obstinate, talkative, complaining and pained are no less right than those who think that he is modest, courageous, intelligent and full of finesse. This is the writer's temperament, allowing him to depict every condition of the human experience, of the human heart.

Whilst the name Dumba epitomises shelter, hospitality, comfort in the face of hostile natural and human-made elements, the name Una constitutes the four-sum of the African cherished qualities of unity, purity, uprightness, humility, vis-a-vis strength in the turbulance of life. Both names draw a lot from the good emulative qualities of the universal ideal personality: selfless, humble, wise, resilient, humorous, patient, incorruptable, exemplary, loyal yet totally independent. The two names epitomise the capability to withstand and endure tempests, the harsh weather, the storms and hurricanes of life. And on top of it the capacity to win against all odds and to celebrate the inevitable success that comes to the brave and valiant.

One

THE GENESIS

It is one o'clock midnight. The night outside is almost pitch black. It is so dark that even the witches would get lost. The whole town is asleep with a few motor bikes snoring away in the distance. But inside a spacious room, in suburbia Midlands, a secret meeting of four persons is being chaired by a small poke-faced bald-headed local politician. His face seems to bear the marks of every sin of personkind. Though calm and composed, behind the exterior lurks an emotional cripple. He is a casualty of a polygamous, unhappy family background that has left his psyche permanently scarred. His face is twisted, by unhappiness, into a shy grin. He is short in stature but long on mischief. If ever there is a creature whose poor adult personality might be excused on the grounds of a traumatic childhood, it is this devil. Some people, and animals, overcome ugliness with charming personalities. Not this devil. He suffers from grave moral flaws: ruthlessness, opportunism, duplicity, egomania, cynicism - above all vengefulness. He is a sinister, wisp of a man, with an intense face and piercing mean, dark eyes. He looks a pretty impoverished human being. He is an emotional cauldron.

He is Mr Trial Makope aged sixty. The meeting has been called by Mr Makope, the chief himself, to discuss and plan a master scheme. The meeting is being conducted with the skill of a master planner and the precision of a field general. His instructions and line of action are given in meticulous detail that would make a field commander grow haggard with envy and awe. There is no doubt as to who the boss is at this meeting. A mild but venomous little man. He is extremely cunning.

The second in command of the operation is a woman, the only woman in this special unit. Ms Arm Zariri is in her late fifties, divorced and hardened She is tempered by personal, social and family battles. Her ex-husband had made a lucky escape. She is fearfully and dangerously superstitious. A hereditary witch, a Jezebel-incarnate, she gets satisfaction and a kick from doing evil. She has a semi-triangular face, like a cat, that makes peals of laughter that sound like opera from ancient graves. Rather more like the laughter of a feeding hyena.

She wears a haggard and mournful face that looks worse for wear. The glasses she wears hide serpentine, and often involuntary weeping, eyes. The glasses seem to be resting on the nose of a cat about to pounce on an unwary mouse. Though huge, plumb and unattractive, she is known to be an athletic, agile and voracious lover when in bed with the chief. Zariri attracts the mating calls of Makope, a small, irate egomaniac with a foul dangerous temper. A dark rather vain man.

These attributes are a bonus, an extra. She need not have any of these attributes, anyway, since the chief is known to go for any creature that is female and answers to the name homo sapiens. Though his virility and reputation as a lover are highly suspect (that of Mr Bang Bang And Roll Over) he has the sexual appetite of a rabbit. Rumour has it that more often than not it is a matter of the spirit willing but the flesh being weak.

Both the woman and the chief share many attributes in character and aptitude. Both have an unbridled brute ambition and a ruthlessness that would make Macbeth and his lady a child's play. Both have divorced in a cruel manner that left the whole town stung, stunned and horrified. Both can kill, and have killed in cold blood. The psychopaths easily pass, with flying colours, as founder members of the Zima Axe Killers' Association.

Makope and Zariri are people ordinary mortals avoid. These two are part of the practitioners of the dark arts. They belong to the night. They are children of darkness, with certain wisdom. They know the secrets of the dark. They go to the night as if to a friend, enter the darkness as if it were a home, as if the black curve of the night were the dome of their dwelling. So the place asssumes the false, concentrated and exaggerated innocence of the truly wicked. Through such people disaster runs and the devil drives.

The other two members of the group have lower but essential ranks in the operation. Pissmore Onda is tallish, strong built, with a babyish face. The short stubbish and round cheeks hide an evil and sadistic streak in his nature. He wishes anyone evil. He ferrets for information with the energy, persistence and accuracy of a sniffer. Hatred, envy, jealousy and malice are second nature to him. It is a psychosis.

The fourth member is Inda Aka. He is short, plumb, in fact round, and has protruding eyes. He is affable but suffers from infantile complexes which can be traced to an unhappy upbringing painfully devoid of a father in the family. He seems to be in constant, perpetual search of a father substitute. He never grows up, he just grows older. He is a typical adult-cum-boy who can be sent on nefarious errands. Hence, he hero-worships and adores the chief, Mr Trial Makope, the local politician.

These four personalities complement each other in such a manner that the operation they are planning would be implemented and executed with almost computer accuracy. At the end of the briefing the chairperson clears his voice. With hate rising like vapour from his eyes, his voice thick with venom he announces in an esoteric manner

'From now on this scheme will be known and referred to, by the four of us, as *Operation Doctor Elimination*, in short *ODE*.[1] He sits back and keeps smiling his infamous mirthless, wolflike grin, while seething inside. Seeing his enemy clearly in his mind he threatens, 'Dumba I'll destroy you. I'm the master of disaster. I'm the terror. After all, young man, you are only a grain of *sand*, of no consequence.'

The four part company. The chief and his lover retire for the night, though it is very late. The other two, Mr Onda and Mr Aka drive away to their homes in Mr Aka's ancient car. It is a jalopy that has seen many a breakdown. It is an appalling little car, with the doors fastened with wire. It is an old heap that rattles, whistles and wheezes in a cloud of smoke. The jalopy coughs, sneezes, splatters and strains towards the two conspirators' homesteads. The four minds have one thing in common, the successful conclusion of *Operation Doctor Elimination*. In short *ODE*. It is strange that these people are united by spite, suspicion, hatred and envy. They whip themselves into a frenzy of hatred and cruelty. The minds and psychology of such people are indeed puzzling.

The following day, at the big general Hospital and Training complex, the Principal Officer Dr Henry Dumba parks his pick-up truck and rushes to his deputy's office to check on some important data. He knocks on the door but there is no answer. He tries the door handle. The door is locked. He checks with the receptionist but to no avail. He goes into his office, tries his deputy's home phone number but there is no reply. The phone rings for a long time but noone answers. The ringing tone buzzes like a monotonous-voiced insect trapped inside the receiver. No reply. He tries again...still no reply. He gives up in exasperation. He runs to the Teaching Hall to check on the examination roll but finds the whole place in chaos. His deputy has let him down yet again.

Nevertheless, being an experienced administrator he manages to bring the situation under control. Years of experience have taught him the essential skills in management by crisis.

The time is now 10:30 a.m. The phone harshly rings in Dr Dumba's office. A female voice asks him to hold on for a call from Mr Makope's office. After what seems to be an eternity, the time lapse that makes your beard grow, Makope comes on the line

'Dumba, this is chief Makope himself. Er young man Ms Zariri, your deputy, is not coming to work today, and tomorrow. Her car has just broken down. I just happen to pass by so she asked me to tell you of her predicament. I hope you will understand. Bye.'

Dumba is speechless. He asks himself aloud how on earth a politician, a local one for that matter, has anything to do with the running of a hospital and training institution. Is Mr Makope trying to tell him something? This unpopular politician is a notorious impulsive womaniser and an infamous meddler. Only last week he was caught on the hospital grounds, literally with his pants down, making love to a toothless hag in his car. The hospital guards could not believe their eyes. Dumba tells himself to forget it and concentrate on his work. You can't waste time on crazy folks like Makope. Folk who belong to the new degeneration age.

After all, Dumba's own friends in the capital city had forewarned him to guard against such Third World characters: the vermin of Africa steeped in corruption. They stop at nothing to get at their prey, or their enemy whether real or imagined. Dumba sharply recalls his superiors' advice when he was transferred on promotion to this Midlands institution. Holding such a senior position in the Midlands is like riding a hungry salivating hyena. You drop your guard or doze off, and make one slight error, you are eaten up. That is the end of you.

African people, no matter how schooled, are tribes-people at heart. They resent bright, successful and hardworking neighbours. If you are successful, you win false friends and true enemies. Dumba's comparative young age, and brilliance would attract the envy, jealousy, spite, wrath and malice of tribespeople like Makope, Zariri and their henchmen. Having Ms Zariri as one's deputy further worsens the situation. It is like walking daily through a minefield. Dining and supping with such a devil would require supernatural skills for one to survive. Add to it characters like Messrs Onda and Aka on the institution's staff and you have a real recipe for machinations and double dealing. It's like sharing a den with venomous vipers.

A long distance call from Headquarters brings Dumba's thoughts back to the issues of his office. He is told that he has been nominated to represent the country at an international conference in Geneva. He has to give a paper on Health Education and Development in Africa. The conference will last a month. Dumba welcomes the offer heartily though with some trepidation. Indeed it gives him yet another chance to mix and share ideas with other world scholars. Such cross-fertilisation of ideas is the very essence of intellectual growth. This is always a refreshing occasion very different from the dreary chores of administrative work.

However, these pleasant sweet thoughts are soured by the realisation that his deputy, Ms Zariri, would have to act in his place. Not only will she conspire at his total downfall but mismanage the institution into a complete mess. All the female staff, students and workers will definitely be at the mercy of Makope, the local chief. The sex maniac will have a free range, a free run, an orgy, for a whole month. The whole institution will return to the Sodom and Gomorrah it was when Zariri acted for some time before his appointment.

Makope has always, of course, dreamt and relished the day Dumba would leave the institution, preferably for good. He, Mr Makope, the chief would perform a jig in the streets and throw a party for everyone in celebration. This would be one of the now rare occasions when he would have the chance to go into a feasting frenzy on women of loose morals given to him on a platter. He may be able to indulge in an occasional act of sodomy. For he is an occasional sodomite too, womaniser aside.

Dumba ponders over these and other possible consequences of his absence from the institution for the month. He shudders at the horrific possibilities. He however, shrugs his shoulders helplessly as he proceeds to prepare for the trip. At this point he remembers his old man's advice

'Cut it out son of Dumba. You can't hope to cleanse the world and the dirty Africa single handed. Son, it's best left to the gods and the unborn. Indeed, the ways of the world are puzzling and those of Africa very perplexing .You see son, the African continent is in the shape of a question mark. It raises more questions than answers. It's a self-afflicted horrendous continent.'

*   *   *   *

It is now 5:30 p.m. Dumba is reminded of the rather late time by the sound of his wife's V.W. beetle going past. She is on her way home from her place of work, a high school just across the stream from the hospital. She has, naturally, noticed her husband's van still parked outside his office. She parks her car and decides to pop in. She knocks on the door lightly, opens it and announces her arrival with a mischievous 'Good morrow Sir!' She gives a delicious little giggle. Her eyes dance flirtingly at him. There are no eyes like those in the world, Dumba observes. With a flick of the arm he checks the time. It is 5:40 p.m. He earnestly thanks her for coming to the rescue. Una smiles and puts her right arm in his to support him as he rises from the chair. He squeezes tight on it, imprisons it as they walk out of the office. He treasures it, guarding it as the eyelid guards the eye

'Henry love. It's not good for your health to overwork yourself. There is always a tomorrow, you know.' Says Una with the air of one who has lived for all time. Dumba agrees resignedly T know, I know. I thought I'd to finish up some of the reports before I leave for the conference. You see.' Una does not respond to this last statement. She takes him to the car park in silence.

She leads the way home in her car as he follows behind in the white Mazda van. As the V.W. beetle speeds on he is rather struck by the beautiful ugliness of the German car. It's rugged, tough yet it looks fragile. Its backside stands out invitingly like that of a dragonfly. Curiously it resembles Ms Zariri's big behind. Makope might be invited by the mating calls of this shaped metal. He might have a bestial erection. Strange thoughts about a car that, when standing, looks like a sleeping tortoise enjoying the hypnotic African sun.

As Una drives along the winding and bumpy road her mind goes back to the conference issue. She knows her husband enjoys international fora especially those concerned with intellectual and academic matters. She is very happy for him. He seems tailor-made for intellectual aggression.

However, she is rather apprehensive at the prospect of sabotage by some of her husband's subordinates at work. They will definitely conspire to dethrone him in his absence. Zariri in particular, would be incited by Makope to work on some dangerous mischief. Only last week Zariri and Makope were seen at MaDube's, the witchdoctor's place shopping for black magic, proper juju, to cast spells on Dr Dumba.

To imagine they went through the ordeal of taking large quantities of snuff. They blew at both ends, sneezed and shed both real and sentimental tears. Throughout the night they sang and danced to the tune of the African drums, and the name of Dumba. They sang their voices hoarse, sprinkling African beer into the air in a passionate effort to draw the wrath of the spirits on Dumba. They stomped the ground to the scathing beat of ox-hide drums until their feet swelled. They shook rattles wildly to the accompaniment of the wailing *thumb piano* invoking the names of Dumba's deceased ancestors. The women's sharp, haunting ululations sliced across this solemn din, in typical juju incantation. The spirits of *Dumbaphobia* , and of hatred, were visibly abroad. They drank, danced and sang themselves silly. Exhausted, they surreptitiously left, at dawn, the witchdoctor's place through the back door.

Though this bizarre event was an open secret, and the talk of the neighbourhood, Una and Henry had not taken it seriously. They had laughed it off as one of the tragedies and paradoxes of modern day Africa. Henry calls it Africa's cross-road to development. It is the scourge and curse of Africa. It is such superstitious beliefs that hinder development. What the Portuguese call *obscurandisimo*. Schooled people spend precious time, energy, money and resources on chasing mirages of superstition. They travel far and wide to consult bones, sticks, calabashes thrown by simple folk in hypnotic trances.

Witchdoctors make a fortune, on foolishness and gullibility, dispensing charms and herbs to be worn under those expensive suits and dresses. Charms and herbs for promotion, protection, luck, success, respect, instilling fear into one's adversaries are all available. Some even commit grisly ritual murders of children or adults in an endeavour to enhance their political, economic or social positions. What a weird world, what a parody. Education has to get rid of this horrific rubbish.

Una is shaken out of the very depressing soliloquy by shouts of joy coming from the direction of their house. Their children have seen them coming. As they get out of the cars they are mobbed in greeting by their children. The din from their voices fills the house as they relate to their parents the events of the day. After a while, the excitement subsides as they settle down to some drinks. Una and the youngsters have tea, coffee, orange juice, and some biscuits. Henry settles down to a cold litre of beer. The youngest of the children sits, as usual, on dad's lap purring contentedly. Occasionally, and curiously, it gives small-nosed double-barrelled sniffs as it pulls at its nectar of orange juice. For the little child this is its spot of happiness, its heaven on earth.

After supper, and the news on television, they all retire for the night but not before Henry listens to the news broadcast from B.B.C: London. It is ironic that one cannot believe and trust the news that comes from home. The local, mainly state-controlled, media distort, doctor, adulterate and distil events until the news is nothing but propaganda and lies.

*   *   *   *

The aeroplane, like a big metallic preying mantis, appears on the horizon, touches down on the runway and taxies ominously towards the airport terminal. As it comes to a halt, small and squared metallic beetles rush to it and surround it. Some push ladders against it while others wait by with their cannons ready. A door near its nose opens and people of all shapes, sizes and colours stream out. Well-wishers, relatives and friends wave and shout at the figures they recognise. The passengers wave back to acknowledge the welcome.

In the welcoming crowd are two but separate parties interested in one of the passengers arriving from Europe. Una and children are there to meet Henry and take him home. They have sorely missed him for the whole month. As he emerges from the plane the small group raise a cheer and give him a rousing welcome. After the immigration and customs formalities they greet, hug him warmly and heartily. They drive home in a jovial and excited mood. In a gale of laughter and good spirits gifts and tokens of far away exotic Europe find their way to Una and the children.

But unknown to them some private eye, in the form of Mr Aka, has surreptitiously watched the whole scene. He has been briefed to watch and check on the arrival of Dr Dumba and to note his movements. A tab must be put and kept on him. Immediately Dumba and family drive off from the airport Aka sprints for the telephone booth to make a long distance call. After the call he flags down a cab and tells the driver to head for the city.

As Aka rides into town he is quite happy with himself. He has managed to keep to the letter of instructions given to him. His mind goes back to the meetings they had held since Dr Dumba left for Europe. They had held three of them, besides the informal briefings. At the third meeting they had been joined by three other people, all of them specialists in their areas of operations.

Mr Lazu is quite experienced in financial matters, especially those concerned with the fiddling of funds. Here is a man warped by life, enfeebled by surrender to greed and lust. Though small in stature, thin, famished and emaciated he has milked away goods and commodities, from the government hospital, worth thousands of dollars. He has conned and framed many an administrator to their peril. He is a master of trickery and cunning. He is always treacherous and resentful.

Because of his experience, and a morbid dislike of meticulous authority, such as exhibited by Dr Dumba at the hospital, he would be an asset in operation *ODE*. Before the regime of Dr Dumba Lazu had, with the active cinnivance of Zariri, looted the institution with impunity. As the finance officer he had juggled and fiddled with figures in such a manner that no auditor would question the books.

Mr Jab is the head of a school that trains teachers in town. He has very peculiar manners. He is always glugging and snorting like a hungry donkey. When upset he gently rolls one buttock off the seat and releases a fart of extraordinary resonance. He then proceeds to fix his large eyes on the offending person, twitching his nostrils and lips as if daring the person to laugh, which makes it worse. For the offending person is invariably about to scream with laughter.

Mr Jab is an avowed tribalist and regionalist who would jump at the throat of anyone who doesn't come from his home area. Besides, he is knowledgeable about misconduct regulations that govern civil servants. He belongs to the Teachers' Union. Like Mr Aka, he comes from a family devoid of a father. In fact, he does not know his paternity. Rumour has it that he is sired by a Mozambican witchdoctor of no fixed aboard. So he finds chief Makope, who hails from his home area, a perfect father substitute. He seems to think that everyone must suffer for this unhappy background of his. Mr Jab is tall, dark in complexion and wears a funereal face. Just a carbon copy of his Mozambican witchdoctor father.

The last but very important member is Mr Pirn who is tallish, oval-headed and brown in complexion. Pirn speaks in a shrill squeaky voice. He, like Makope, is a man of vices and debauchery. Though unintelligent he uses his shrill voice to persuade and incite. In this connection he is indefatigable. So he is quite handy as special adviser when it comes to machinations and plots. Like messrs Makope and Jab, he hails from the same area.

Mr Aka recalls how they, as a group, whipped up themselves into a mould of determined cruelty. As far as he, Mr Aka, is concerned, he confesses to himself, he has very little to gain from the demise of Dr Dumba. It is more of spite or rather a morbid desire to please chief

Makope who has acted like a father to him. His role is that of a scorpion that stings a frog for fun. Strange isn't ?

His thoughts are interrupted by the cab pulling up at the bus terminus. Aka scrambles out rather absent-mindedly. He heads for the bus which destination is the Midlands town. He must be back at base in time. Yes the scorpion must be ready for the frog when it arrives.

Two

THE ARREST

It is Friday June 3, 1988. It is more than three years since Dr Dumba has been head of the Hospital and Training Institution. To date he has stamped his mark, authority and character on the institution and its products. The university, as the certificating authority, the government as the financing power, the community at large, patients and students have expressed admiration, appreciation of, and satisfaction with, Dr Dumba's leadership and administration of the institution. In fact, he is a phenomenon. He has so far more than survived the onslaught of plots and machinations from Ms Zariri, Messrs Makope, Onda, Aka, Lazu, Jab and Pirn. The success of Dr Dumba in his work, and the hitherto failure of the plots, leads to the chagrin of the seven conspirators. This fuels the fire of hatred in them. This time, it looks, they have woven an intricate and foolproof trap for Dumba. He cannot escape from it. Operation ODE is on full power and is put into action with resolute determination.

Two hours after Dr Dumba's arrival at his home the police arrive to greet him with a warrant of arrest. The team is led by superintendent Offer Aiwa with a detective inspector Nika to beef up his operations. In typical military fashion Dr Dumba is rudely summoned to CID Police headquarters for questioning on a number of unspecified allegations. Horrified, Dumba protests vehemently as he demands to know the nature and source of the allegations. Before he could raise his lawyer the police enter the premises. They search high, low and wide watched by a puzzled and frightened family.

They bundle Dumba into their car and head for their CID offices. As they approach their offices they shoot past heading for Dumba's parents' farm 22 kilometres out of town. They reach their desired destination within a short time. As the police unceremoniously proceed to search the premises surprise turns to anger and hostility at the flagrant disregard for basic human rights as well as privacy. The old folks open up a barrage of protests, disgust mixed with insults. The police continue with their work undeterred.

Again finding nothing of substance to hang the charges on to, they retreat into a corner of the property, out of ear-range, for a mini-conference. They come back again, this time in a teasing and aggressive manner. Everyone present is quizzed on their daily activities, favourite food; the times they go to the toilet; prices and sources of equipment, items, receipts and invoices, even those for the dogs and cats present. After the harrowing experiences, sometimes comical, the police decide to leave. All the same, they take Dr Dumba with them, ostensibly to give him a lift back home.

But in town they take him straight to their CID offices for further questioning and a statement. There, Dumba endures the gauntlet of interrogations, the persistent threats, pleadings, the carrot-and-stick tactics, the sadistic humour. He fends off the questions with condescension and measured bellicosity born of innocence and indignation.

Meanwhile in the distant rooms he could hear ear-piercing screams, cries and groans of victims under brutal interrogation. The air is filled with torture and tense with fear. His tormentors remind him, rather too openly, that with the prevailing State Of Emergency Regulations the police have widespread and sweeping powers to do anything they please with anyone. This has been the position since 1965 when the Whites, under Muzungu, were in power. The present Socialist government, though African run, has happily carried on with the repressive apparatus. They believe the state of emergency regulations meet the people's aspirations. All events reflect that people are at peace in their hearts. Because of it, their livelihoods and social order are guaranteed. The police are glad to operate it on difficult persons such as Dumba. The conversation is in the local language

'You see Dumba,' came in Supt Aiwa, picking at his large nose, 'You are wasting your time and our time. We all know you fought the liberation war as a freedom fighter and I fought against you on the side of the white regime. That is now irrelevant and immaterial. I killed under, and for, the whites and got my promotion. For your information I got my even bigger promotion under the African majority government for doing the same hell of a good, or bad, job depending on which side of the political fence you are, my dear doctor. People thought that voting in the Africans would end the war and the killings. The killings continue but this time legally, you see.' The well decorated officer pauses for effect and continues in a pompous tone. The tenor of voice and tone associated with the victorious

'You see, the lawyers are ineffective against us. In fact they have no balls. They are, as a matter of fact, after your money. They know, and I know, that you will go to jail no matter how innocent you are. People are imprisoned, my dear doctor, on contrived charges. In this part of the world it is prudent to buy the services of the police or those of the trial magistrate instead of those of a lawyer.'

Dumba protests vigorously, with all the power at his command

That is a damn lie, the legal system in this country... the courts will protect me since I am innocent. Totally innocent. You yourself know it. God knows the son of Dumba is innocent. Everyone knows it.' Dumba pronounces amid bouts of laughter from the detectives present.

'You don't understand how we work Dumba!' Aiwa interjects rather sympathetically. The kind of sympathy normally reserved for the young, the uninitiated, the inexperienced. Aiwa explains further

'You see. We work very closely with the magistrate court, the public prosecutor and in particular the presiding magistrate. They are all our people. We are one and the same. In your case it is even worse because, one, your subordinates will grease the palms of the trial magistrate. Two, the local political chief will make sure the trial magistrate toes the desired line. Moreover, it is an open secret that justice can be bought or hired to destroy an opponent.' He pauses to make sure that the words sink slowly but surely into Dumba's mind.

He is about to continue with his uninvited lecture when Dumba firmly disagrees

'I've every confidence in the impartiality of the courts in this country. I've fought for justice in this country.' He is cut short by an as-a-matter-of-fact announcement from an exasperated Aiwa

'We are not making progress, are we ? We will see Dumba, we will see. Want to take a bet on it ?'

He nonchalantly produces a typed paper for Dumba to read and sign. Dumba cannot believe his eyes. He is being made to sign a statement incriminating himself to charges of fraud involving a sum of $14000 at his place of work. The funds, it is alleged, were supposed to be used for an irrigation scheme for the institution but he had converted it to his own use. Dumba throws back the piece of paper to Aiwa in disgust.

Dumba, however, reflects and quickly decides to talk to these people with calm objectivity. Under the cruellest stress and pressure he remains in charge. He permits himself a smile

'Look, there's no point in arguing over this. I'll have to talk to my lawyer first. Can I take the piece of paper with me?' Dumba looks up at Aiwa. To his relief, the supt gives in but retains the paper.

'You can see your lawyer. We give you two hours to do it . But remember you are wasting your time and money. You learned people are very funny.

You hold these strange foreign ideas about your whiteman's justice. Let me tell you one thing straight. These local magistrates we have in our courts are a slight improvement on your villagers in the kangaroo courts during your war of liberation. They are young, inexperienced, unsophisticated and poor. Not very different from the simple tribesperson. You see they have barely 3 O'levels. They have only received a nine month crash course at the local agricultural centre. So they are open to all sorts of influences and pressures. This is Africa my poor friend, not Europe, not England.' Aiwa sneezes like a bored she-goat.

With this bizarre and fateful lecture Dumba is given leave to go, under police escort, and see his lawyer. After about four short hours Dumba is formally charged and bailed on condition he pays $500 and surrenders all his travel documents. On top of that he has to report to the police once a week.

What perplexes Dumba is the speed and haste with which the latter process has taken. It seems as though all things have been preprogrammed. Furthermore, the presiding magistrate, Mr Igneous Mugo, looks harmless, and indifferent but has physical features very similar to Pissmore Onda's. The round blown up cheeks, the sluggish movements, the subtle, shy peering look, the surreptitious glance are all there. Could it be biological coincidence with deceiving similarities? He wonders.

Also bewildering is the fact that the case and issue do not involve in any way his employers. That is his government ministry or the Public Service Commission. The mystery deepens when the ministry authorities write to Dumba enquiring into the circumstances surrounding the whole affair. Dumba responds by informing them about his own surprise at the allegations and their falsity. As Dumba returns to duty at the institution a high-powered board of inquiry, set up by the ministry, arrives to investigate the issue. Parallel to it is a team of auditors to check on the finances and assets of the hospital as well as the whole institution. Dumba is given a clean bill; nothing is found amiss.

However, the inquiry uncovers an elaborate, sinister and malicious conspiracy, targeted at Dumba, by his subordinates but masterminded by an outsider, a local political chief. Makope's hidden, invisible hand of mischief could be perceived behind the whole sorry sordid affair. The authorities have no option but to take disciplinary action on the conspirators. They are warned, cautioned and transferred from the institution. Messrs Onda and

Aka find themselves in an institution 600 kilometres away. Ms Zariri and Mr Lazu are catapulted 300 kilometres away. All this is, of course, done for the professional good of the institution.

On their part the authorities contact the CID police in an effort to stop the unwarranted prosecution of the very innocent Dr Dumba since the allegations are false and baseless. It takes the CID police four weeks to respond by summoning instead, Dumba to appear in court to face charges as previously laid down. Under the notorious state of emergency regulations and their arbitrary provisions the police can proceed with a case, whether real or imagined, with impunity.

The logic, in this illogical bizarre affair, is that s/he who wields local power cannot afford to be seen to be losing. A little research, by determined adversaries, into the widespread powers given to the police provides ready ammunition and deadly fire-power for the destruction of intransigent victims like Dumba. Acquiescing court officials facilitate the personal vindictive persecutions, on quite a regular basis. The rule of selective and partial law reigns.

It is ironic and tragic that those who suffer this kind of perverted justice are the innocent yet the very useful professional people the country can ill-afford to lose. Inspite of repeated protests from the ministry concerned the police and court officials press on with the charges against Dumba with a religious fanatic zeal. Witnesses are scouted for and engaged in a meticulous mischievous manner. Coaching clinics are given to the witnesses under the careful eye of chief Makope, the baron and his aides as operation ODE is manoeuvred on course. Inevitably, and as planned, Dumba is finally charged with sixteen counts of alleged fraud involving a revised figure of $10000.

Three

THE TRIAL

'Silence in court!' The court orderly's voice booms in the packed courtroom. The presiding magistrate is Mr Igneous Mugo. He enters the courtroom pompously, and conspicuously sits in the chair. He is a ferret faced oaf. He wears a cheap jumble sale suit mercifully shrouded by a ceremonial gown. The gown gives him some air of importance and pseudo-learning.

The prosecution is being handled by a Mr Andreas Mire, a lean, famished and slight man. He wears a hangman's face with a rather cruel, spiteful mouth. His trousers, having endured many a tough year, sport worn patches around the calves. They are secured to his waist by a leather strap that looks more of a leather whip than a belt. His corduroy jacket hangs lazily from his shoulders as he attempts to straighten its many wrinkles with rather involuntary movements of his upper torso.

Dumba's lawyer, Mr Rajiv Thakor, sits next to the prosecutor. His wisened and alert eyes run expertly through a pile of papers infront of him. He looks the more dignified and composed.

Dumba is in the dock. In his well cut suit he looks more of an executive than a defendant in a courtroom. He is calm, pensive and relaxed. His wife, relatives, well-wishers as well as evil-wishers sit rather uneasily in the crowded court room. Journalists from the national media, newspapers, radio and television are all poised with their pens, paper and cocked ears. Invited, and cajoled by Trial Makope, the local chief, rather than driven by professional curiosity, they are ready for a perfunctory coverage of the well orchestrated trial. The trial, which is to last weeks, is a sinister farce and a travesty of justice.

In the extreme left corner of the court-room sit, huddled together, two ancient women, one white and the other black. Next to them crouches a man with roots and medicines in a parcel, hidden inside a lady's basket. These people are to become a permanent feature of every session of the trial. They have been hired by Ms Zariri and company, and financed by a Roman Catholic nun, a white missionary from the US, to cover the proceedings.

The nun, plump and piggish, has a dislike for Dumba which motive is difficult to fathom. Most probably, she detests him because she is a close personal friend of Zariri. She is no lady, in fact she is no religious lady but a hypocrite. She makes one wonder why some people join the holy order. For she delights in seeing people suffer. She takes after her mentor Lucifer. She worships her lord: Satan. Hence, she spends so much energy, time , resources, prayer effort and money plotting horrific deeds. Instead of being a good example of love, forgiveness and constructiveness she is the epitome of vindictiveness, revenge and hatred. She fans these with the same religious zeal that ostensibly brought her into the nunnery. At times it is strange that the truth sounds stranger than fiction for she is indeed the sister of darkness and a messenger of evil. She is known to have said publicly for all to hear that she does not believe in giving the other cheek but in taking out two teeth for one tooth and two eyes for one eye. It's weird.

Mr Andreas Mire, the prosecutor, opens the state case in a persistent but jumbled manner. As he calls his first witness the proceedings are brought to a halt when the defence counsel, Mr Rajiv Thakor, wants to know who the complainant is; who has suffered prejudice. After a lengthy and heated debate, the presiding magistrate rules that, inspite of the lack of a complainant, the hearing should continue. Mr Thakor gives in under protest. So the Judas moment comes. And Dumba must go through with it.

The prosecutor calls in Zariri as the first state witness. She states that she does not know much about the alleged missing funds. The bursar, Lazu, would be in a better position to explain. Under meticulous cross-examination by the defence counsel, she openly admits that Trial Makope, the local political chief, is behind the scheme to have Dr Dumba incriminated. It is the chief who reported the matter to the CID police.

She further admits having a special intimate relationship with the chief whom she finds very warm and comforting. In fact she loves Makope so much that his wish is her command. She also makes a damning confession that being Dumba's deputy she stands to benefit from his downfall. She goes on to say that she does not like Dumba; in fact she strongly detests his appointment, 'recycling[1], to the institution. That is why Makope, Lazu, five others and herself have decided to frame up Dumba.

These revelations and other confessions are greeted by the large audience in court with gasps of disbelief and disgust.

Undeterred, but now sweating and frothing at the mouth, she goes further to reveal that they, as a group, have decided to take the case upon themselves because they feared that Dumba's friends at the ministry head office, the minister included, would protect him.

At this point Dumba's father, sitting in the audience, looks around for an open window, evidently intent on spitting out his disgust. But on second thoughts he marches out in protest, never to come again to such a court of injustice. To the old man this is a circus.

Mr Thakor proceeds to thank Ms Zariri for such a ferocious and shameless self-confession; for telling the court that it is a frame up, a trumped-up charge based on hatred, greed, malice, envy and brute ambition.

Next to go into the witness box is Lazu. In an unusual calmness he relates how the non-existent fund exists by twisting the facts such that the defence counsel intervenes on many occasions in an effort to follow the grain of his testimony. Lazu stretches the truth to its utmost breaking point. He is asked to show the court the books, the balance sheets, the bank accounts, assets registers relating to the alleged account.

He admits he has none of the items asked for except his memory and fertile imagination, concluded Mr Thakor. Asked why he, Lazu, and Zariri took it upon themselves to take the matter to the police, Lazu parrots the same answer as Zariri's. He also admits that he strongly dislikes Dr Dumba and wants to see him removed from the institution. He sits down without being asked to do so. Everyone in the courtroom is surprised at the sudden stop in giving evidence. Mr Thakor prods him to go on but he remains seated and silent.

Incredibly the circus of injustice continues. Inspite of the absurdity of this testimony, and inspite of the totally justified protestations of the defence counsel, more witnesses are called upon to testify. Next come witnesses from alleged sources of the funds. Again nothing much of substance comes out of them. They all refer to some remote possibilities of a fund existing between their companies and Dumba's institution.

When cross-examined by the defence counsel, they eventually admit that the funds belong to the companies who informally donated funds and goods to whoever requested them from the institution. One of the white managers informs the court that all of the alleged missing funds are in fact back on their books. He cannot say for sure who paid in the money except that he found the books balancing.

The African manager of the other company is almost incoherent. He cannot separate the said account from the rest of his own accounts. Like his counterpart in the other company, he could not tell who asked for, or collected, the funds. All he could remember is that some monies should have somehow got to the institution.

The next state witnesses, six of them, come from firms that, the prosecution claims, sold items to Dumba using the alleged funds. Here is a mixed confused bag. Some emphatically recall Dumba coming to their shops to collect items they cannot remember. Others are honest enough to tell the court that they have had no dealings whatsoever with Dumba. More witnesses are called but they do not help the prosecution's case.

After ten postponements and remands, the prosecutor becomes desperate. Mire becomes more vindictive and cunning. Further witnesses are hired on their ability and willingness to incriminate Dumba at all costs. But under the superb cross-examination by Mr Thakor they relent and show through their complicity in the case against Dumba. Last come the CID police officers, supt Aiwa and detective inspector Nika. They say a lot to help the defence case. They have no exhibits to show. However, they observe that they had seen some structures at Dumba's parents' farm, which materials they thought came from the firms. Again under cross-examination the two police officers agree that Dumba's parents had shown them receipts for the materials they had suspected of being stolen.

Seven sittings and two postponements later, Mire the prosecutor, his spirits and enthusiasm dampened, closes the case. Mr Thakor in his usual brilliant manner tears apart the prosecution's case so far. He formally applies to the court for the case to be dismissed since there is absolutely no case to answer. The prosecution has failed to show the court any evidence to prove the existence of the alleged fund both at the institution and at the two companies. There is no complainant nor prejudice. An official investigation and an audit report have given Dr Dumba a clean bill. All the institution's funds and assets are there and can be accounted for. In fact no such account as alleged exists at the institution.

Mr Thakor directs the court's attention to the evidence of Zariri and Lazu when they categorically stated that the whole issue is a frame up born of greed, envy, malice and hatred. The prosecution has failed to produce any item as exhibit before the court. The two concerned companies' books are in fact balancing. None of their funds are missing. In all fairness and honesty, the learned lawyer asserts, the court cannot put the accused on his defence. It would be like asking him to prove his own innocence. The lawyer asks the court to acquit Dumba on all the counts as charged.

At this point the presiding magistrate, Igneous Mugo, tells Dumba to stand up. Mugo hesitates, and to the bewilderment of everyone in court he decides to continue with the case. Without giving any reasons he rules that Dumba be put on his defence. Yet again the trial is postponed for two weeks, to the surprise of everyone. Such are the strange workings of adulterated justice.

*   *   *   *

Two weeks later the trial resumes with Dumba giving his evidence-in-chief. Like in the defence outline, he denies all the charges. It has been his first time to hear of the existence of the nameless alleged account. As far as he is concerned it is fictitious, an invention of his enemies. He goes on to produce the audit and exchequer act, the financial handbooks to prove his points. The same documents spell out duties and functions of the head of institution, in this case Dr Dumba. He is the accounting officer, accountable to head office. Subordinates like Zariri and Lazu are accountable as well as answerable to Dumba.

Mr Trial Makope has absolutely nothing to do with the affairs of the institution. Dumba proceeds to produce several letters and memos from Makope to certain influential politicians, the country's president included, alleging misconduct on the part of Dumba as head of the hospital and training institution. Dumba tells the court the history and catalogue of malicious machinations as well as abortive plots spearheaded by Makope, Lazu and Zariri. All aimed at toppling Dumba from the headship of the institution. The case in court is part of the continuing intrigue and complicity against him. He also produces written evidence from his employers, the ministry and public service commission, indicating that they too are at a loss as to what the case is all about. As far as they know nothing is missing from the hospital and training institution. As a matter of fact they are very happy with Dumba's administration.

The defence closes its case. The prosecution's turn to make its submission comes. Mire sums up his case in under a minute. It is a brief surprising pronouncement. He claims that the prosecution's case is clear. He sits down.

20

The defence counsel, Mr Thakor, makes his submission that lasts an hour and half. He goes through the case with a legal tooth comb. He carefully and meticulously covers every count, every allegation and every witness' evidence. He weighs every gram of evidence submitted so far.

He tells the court that some people at some time have been wrongly suspected of something.

'Solely on the basis of suspicion, born of hatred or sheer malice, people are dragged before the courts. The question must be asked, why should some people at some point in time actually want someone to have done something that they condemn; even to the extent of creating it. In the history of the courts *innocent* people have erroneously been convicted on false evidence, trumped-up charges, on carefully manipulated testimony of malicious people. Dr Dumba's case is a textbook example of a well planned and executed plot to incriminate an innocent, law-abiding professional person.'

'Evidence has been led before the court to prove that this is a frame up by a handful of powerful and resolute enemies of the accused. We have heard here, your worship, Ms Zariri and Mr Lazu tell us loud and clear 'Yes it was a frame up...Yes we hated him...Yes it was Makope who reported the matter to the CID police!'

'So it is loud and clear that this case before us is a conspiracy, a plot, a frame up against the innocent law-abiding Dumba. There is no doubt about that. Your worship, we live in difficult times. The history, and story, of life has never been smooth. People are, and can be mischievous. These people accusing Dumba are that kind of people: dirty, cruel, mean, mischievous bastards.'

To convict the accused on the basis of what has transpired in this courtroom smacks of the biblical Herodian justice: 'Let the innocent die lest the guilty escape!' Or rather it is the logic of the cannibal: 'When there is no one to eat, eat the one put before you.'

'Justice which does not subscribe to the perennial dictum that the prosecution must prove its case beyond any shadow of doubt, beyond any reasonable doubt, is not justice at all. Rather, it is a deal worked out between the members of a single, privileged law enforcement agency. It is akin to state collective oppression. It is state sponsored terror. This is the opportune moment to say no to this kind of perverted justice, the right occasion to say no to state terror. The correct platform to announce that the courts of this noble land dispense true justice without fear or favour, without looking over their shoulders in case the powers-that-be disapprove.'

'Your worship, gentlewomen and gentlemen, you can only protect your liberties in this world by protecting the other person's freedom. You can only be free if I am free, if he is free. The same thing that would get him may be used to get you. It could be the beginning of tyranny. Today it is him, tomorrow it is me, and you! And the system that is not strong enough, courageous enough, to protect all its people, all its citizens ought not to live upon the face of the earth.'

'Your worship,' the lawyer concludes, 'I repeat the prosecution has dismally failed to prove its case beyond reasonable doubt. In fact the prosecution is asking this honourable court to preside over, and put its stamp of approval on, a fabricated, vindictive story. A sorry story of a private personal grudge, a vendetta brought about by people who should be adult enough to know what is fair, and what is right. People who are in cahoots. As a court of justice we should refuse to be part of this vendetta. We should send a clear message to everyone that we say no to this puerile nonsense.'

'Your worship, it is our sincere, humble but emphatic submission that the accused be found innocent and acquitted on all counts as charged.'

There is tumultuous spontaneous applause from the audience, presspersons included, as Mr Thakor resumes his seat.

The presiding magistrate, Mr Mugo, yet again postpones the case for four weeks to allow himself enough time to study the case before passing judgement. As people leave the court-room they comment openly and loudly that Dumba is innocent. Even the public prosecutor, Andreas Mire concedes openly that the prosecution has lost the case. Disappointed he asks a junior colleague of his to cover for him the proceedings on judgement day.

*   *   *
*

Soon the word, like rumour, begins to spread and feed on itself. It spreads and spreads. It moves, and moves faster than wind. It, like a flame, leaps in leaps and bounds ahead of its carrier. The courier meets it before s/he delivers the message. It is now talk of the town. It is on everyone's lips. It is spoken in different languages, strange tongues and in local dialects. Queues form outside Mr Thakor's offices for an appointment by those seeking his special talented word, his legal services.

Four

FATE BE KIND

The word also swiftly reaches chief Makope and company through the usual court couriers, the winds of gossip, rumour and exaggeration. The party of collaborators panics and so convenes hurriedly. Fears of failure, possible costly lawsuits, mixed with spite lead to desperation. The desperation is written all over their faces as they sit round the table. A quick and unanimous decision is reached. ODE must succeed at all costs. Dumba must be convicted and jailed, this time by crook, not by hook. The fish has stubbornly, wisely and cleverly refused to take the hook disguised as the bait. It has refused to bite at all. The fish has not even attempted a bite. The presiding magistrate, like the prosecutor, should be having problems. Some persuasion, overt and covert, is found necessary if success in the operation is to be realised. So the carrot and stick method has to be used, by all means, on the now rather reluctant presiding magistrate; and the seemingly failing public prosecutor.

It is agreed that a sum of $6000 should be found from the members present. The catholic American white nun quickly chips in with several dollars for a holiday abroad for two. Onda, Pirn and Lazu are tasked to approach the presiding magistrate with the irresistible offers. Chief Makope will lean on him to add extra weight to make sure he does the wanted things to the letter of instruction. So through favour and fear he should toe the desired line. Onda, as the blood cousin to Mugo, will drive home the inherent benefits vis-a-vis the potential hazards of failure to cooperate in this their hour of need. For them indeed the hour has come.

Furthermore, the services of the supernatural world have to be secured, to make victory certain. The conspirators take out an additional insurance. They have to visit the witchdoctor. Zariri and Aka would be led by Jab to a distant but well known witchdoctor of Malawian origin. This man with some unpronounceable name is reputed to have the strongest, the most powerful and potent medicines that would ensure Dumba's conviction and obvious incarceration. The *muti* would guarantee his imprisonment.

It is agreed that money for consultation and procurement of the *muti* will have to come from Zariri and Lazu who have given evidence in court against Dumba. It is believed this link would further strengthen as well as enhance the sorcery powers of the *juju* . In parts of Africa bad luck and misfortune always have a cause. Bad luck and misfortune are sent deliberately by fellowpersons or by the victim's displeased ancestral spirits. A person's fate or fortune is strongly associated with the general relationship supposed to exist between a person and the spirits of deceased ancestors. So through a judicious use of sorcery and invocation to the intended victim's ancestral spirits, a reputable witchdoctor would bring absolute disaster to the unfortunate targeted person.

As Zariri, Aka and Jab enter the witchdoctor's hut they take off their shoes. Together they noisily partake of the snuff mixed with marijuana offered to them. This particular witchdoctor's preferred method of divination involves staring vacantly into a special oily calabash and a duiker horn containing medicines dripping with castor oil.

He sits back on his heels, rearranges his skin cloak, unscrews the stopper of the snuff-horn that hangs around his neck. He proceeds to pour brown snuff into the palm of his hand and draws it up each nostril. He sneezes ecstatically with tears running down his withered old cheeks. He spits into the open fire. His spittle hits the embers of the fire with a spluttering hiss. After a while he announces his findings in a lilting sing-song voice hoarse with emotion.

'Dumba, the potential victim, has very powerful and protecting family spirits. His travels and studies in Europe have toughened him immensely. This is his strongest line of defence. His unbreakable backbone. His other strongest line of defence is that he is an innocent man.' The witchdoctor gives a word of warning. 'Harmful charms cast on an innocent person are known to have a boomerang effect on the user, in this particular case on Zariri, the initiator. With hard luck she may end up a doormat-chewing schizophrenic.' Thus he gives his prophecy, his summation with relish and knowing glances at the clients, as if to say 'the oracle has spoken'. This notwithstanding, an hour's persuasion, a one hundred dollar payment and a bundle of mixed medicines seal the deal.

Nevertheless, before returning to base, the trio decide to consult a second witchcraft opinion, just in case. They drive swiftly fifty kilometres to the east of the first witchdoctor's home. As they approach the second witchdoctor's homestead an assistant goes out to meet them. The witchdoctor-diviner provides hospitality to the clients, in a separate hut, before making his divination. This hut is readily located by its smell. Arranged on woven mats is a vast array of rotting bits of wildlife: the heads of dogs, cats, lizards, bats, monkeys and assorted baboons. Hides, pickled snakes and elephants' testicles are all for sale. Business can be brisk. The diviner has a keen eye on money.

The diviner keeps a sharp ear on, and close surveillance of, his clients. He and his assistants are most likely helped by a certain amount of eavesdropping. You see, the diviner is supposed to be able to tell the clients what their problem is before they say anything to him or her.

Eventually the trio are taken into the consultation hut where the diviner is already going into a trance. He bellows, twitches, shakes violently and vibrates uttering, intermittently, sharp cries drowned in moans. These are followed by the blood curdling ululations of women present.

This diviner combines two methods of divination: the trance and the use of a calabash on a string. One end of the string is fastened to the roof of his hut, and the other held by the diviner. He throws the calabash up as he asks the question put to him. And the answer depends on whether the calabash stays up or comes straight down again. In reality, and to a careful observer, it is controlled by the diviner since it depends on how taut he holds the string.

The diviner moves swiftly and unobstrusively to the possession trance again. This is a remarkable feat. He makes his first statements deliberately vague, and keeps talking sometimes in an ancient dialect, becoming more and more precise while the clients remain silent or react positively depending on how close to the mark the diviner's statement is.

The diviner is able to tell the delegation the reason for their errand and what they want to hear. He does so through an astute assessment, perhaps unconscious and aided by a heightened awareness induced by the possession trance, of their reactions and feedback as he feels his way with his statements. His divination is also helped greatly by the surveillance done early on as the clients waited in the medicine kiosk (hut).

The diviner confirms their wishes and desires. He foretells that Dumba will definitely be convicted and jailed for five years, no matter how innocent he is. Provided they do four things. One, they use properly the concoction of roots, bark, hairs of apes he gives them. Two, they should buy the support of the trial magistrate. Three, a powerful chief must bend the magistrate in the required direction. Four, On the night before the trial, Zariri and Mrs Lazu should have an all night vigil, seated naked in a pond of chilled water chanting the names of Dumba and his family spirits.

With this the diviner conies to the end of the seance. He goes outside the hut alone, and comes out of the trance with a sharp cry. It is a cry that sounds like that of a tortured cat. Or that of a cat that has stepped on to a red-hot hearth stone by error. The cry seems to die in his throat. The cry dies abruptly, as though the person that utters it has been suddenly strangled.

The delegation of three pays for the services rendered. They depart armed with the expensive bundle of evil charms in the kit. This time they are fully satisfied. The oracle of fate and disaster has spoken. With all this magical and cultural weaponry Dumba has no chance.

*   *   *   *

But at times strange things happen. Things without explanation. Things that defy logic. Just five kilometres from the diviner's homestead, the trio are caught in a lashing storm that comes literally from the blue. Suddenly the sky thickens with flashes of lightning and bursts of thunder. There is a sudden darkness everywhere. The clouds, turning white and then black, gather rapidly. The leading clouds, lowering and black as soot-laden smoke, drive with extraordinary swiftness across the sky. There is a glare of light, the whole earth seems on fire, and the vault of heaven cracks overhead.

Terrified, the trio stop the car in the middle of the track. The singing and crying of insects and birds ceases, happiness and excited talk change to fear. Are the gods and Dumba's ancestral spirits angry with them, they muse. Are their own ancestral spirits angry at what they are doing to the innocent Dumba? Are these the signs of worse things to come? The freak storm replies with ear-splitting claps of thunder.

A tree nearby is uprooted and tossed in their direction crushing the front part of the car. Tension rapidly grows among the occupants of the car. Absolute silence falls. It is a silence in which you could hear your own blood flowing. You could almost hear the heavy clouds drifting about in the air. Even the stubborn flies inside the car take cover under the passengers' armpits.

26

The atmosphere changes. A whistling breaks the hurting and frightening silence and redoubles itself. The atmosphere, the air, becomes saturated with rain and is too heavy to breathe. Now the wind blows with such violence that the car rocks perilously from side to side as if it is riding waves on a rough sea. A loose front bumper is blown off and waves goodbye to the rest of the car. Thunder, lightning and rain prevail. The wind proceeds to occupy the car, snatching dusty rugs from the dashboard sweeping it bare. The parcel of roots, bark, rotting hair ad infinitum drops to the floor spilling its contents all over the car. The odour they release mixes with the thick moist air inside the car resulting in a suffocating smog. The air is rendered unfit, unclean for human breathing.

Through the now gaping windows the lightning-lit scene outside is momentarily clearly visible. In the surrounding bushes the creepers which before had looked like cobwebs now stream up into the sky to plead with the ferocious clouds. The bushes are laid flat on the ground as closely as a rabbit lays back its ears. Loosened branches leap about in the sky. As the wailing wind moves it tosses things up on its tail, like a schizophrenic chasing nothing. The rain-laden wind whistles by whilst trees bend to let it pass. All creatures, great and small, pay homage of fear to this freak, mad, livid storm.

The whirling and torrential storm lasts half an hour but to the car occupants it is a long frightening ordeal. After half an hour, like magic, things return to normal. Everything clears up again and life returns to the area again.

The delegation of three emerge from the car and abandon it. It has been immobilised by the storm. The invisible hand of fate, of nature has dealt it a blow. They, and it, have received a terrible knock from the unseen fists of the supernatural.

They paddle through water, in some places knee deep, and brave the slippery and treacherous ground. They walk for close on ten kilometres to reach the nearest bus stop. They are dead tired. They are hungry and exhausted.

Five

THE INJUSTICE

It is July 26, the day Mr Mugo, the presiding magistrate, gives judgement. The packed court-room is bursting at the seams. Its contents of people spills over and out into the corridors. As they jostle for seats and vantage points the court orderly, shouting at the top of his lungs, orders those without seats to leave the room. The pair of hags huddle as usual in the corner nursing a basket whose contents are crucial to the outcome of the case in point. The man, in the company of the hags, guards jealously the fateful *juju* parcel in the basket.

The court rises as the trial magistrate enters the room. Strangely and curiously he takes quite some time to settle down. He dithers, arranges and rearranges the wards of paper on his desk. He looks dazed, uncomfortable and heavily overhung. He seems to be subconsciouly fighting an internal battle. Sometimes it takes as much courage not to do a thing as to do it. To be just or not to be is the question, it seems. Moreover, Dumba is his first accused with a doctorate degree. He cannot afford to let him free, just for the record. Just for the prestige of having imprisoned a PhD holder is great for him. But the most pressing things are the pressure from those quarters, the financial gains, the possible consequences of not cooperating. The fellow seems to be in emotional turmoil.

After the long pause, Mugo picks up courage, clears his voice to address the court. He heaves a heavy audible sigh as if he is trying to off load an unbearable load. Is he wrestling with his conscience, one wonders. Eventually, in a slow, punishing manner he plods through his handwritten notes. He can hardly read what he has written himself. Could it be anxiety, illiteracy or both? The laborious ancient task of recording court proceedings has been done in long hand by Mugo himself.

The archaic, primitive and inaccurate method of recording reveals its faults in many forms. Names of witnesses are all mixed up. Pertinent evidence led in court is left out. Poor English expression and appalling language difficulties cloud and distort facts. Dr Dumba's gender is changed to feminine as he is repeatedly referred to as 'she' and 'her'.

The painful pace, the incomprehensible style, the semi-literate approach, the court ritual learnt by rote, and now applied

28

inappropriately, the two hours send, mercifully, the audience to sleep. Impervious to the snores and dozing he rumbles on, twisting and mixing fact upon fact in the wanted direction.

Now tired from the effects of the self-inflicted ordeal, and of alcohol, he winds up illogically with the announcement that he has to find Dumba guilty of the 15 counts as charged by the prosecution. 'Dumba,' the magistrate asserts, 'has failed to prove his innocence. Moreover, it is better that nine innocent people go to jail rather than allow one possible guilty person to go free.' Mugo himself has decided to believe Zariri and Lazu. 'Zariri's reference to a frame-up has been only a slip of the tongue. The reports from Dumba's employers and the auditors he personally finds them irrelevant.'

There is pandemonium in the courtroom. There is lamentation. Shouts and gasps of utter disbelief at the injustice reverberate from the audience. The press, observers and even the acting public prosecutor, are caught off-guard. There is rhubarb as well as unprintable comments from several groups in the courtroom. All directed at Mugo, who almost shouting, remands Dumba, out of custody, for two weeks. He is to come back for mitigation and sentence. Before the court orderly tells the court to rise and be silent, rather perfunctorily and unnecessarily, Mugo beats a hasty retreat back into the chambers.

It is most charitable to describe mugo's performance as amateurish, incompetent, unethical, arbitrary if not immoral. What a mockery and a caricature of justice. It leaves all thinking, reasonable people stunned. So much for the law...and so little for justice.

But the session ends on a tragicomedy. A surreal drama of mixed tragic and comic events comes to life as a new commotion bursts in the corner where the trio have been seated. Somehow, the fateful basket has been accidentally or otherwise knocked over by the people rushing out. The bizarre contents of the parcel in the basket have been spilled and exposed for all to see when the man dives frantically for the basket. In the process he inadvertently butts the old white woman from behind. She is knocked on her back where she stays for a few moments, kicking like a baby, and rotating from the momentum of the impact. Their partner, the old black woman, freezes in her footsteps opening her mouth in a silent scream. The white hag quickly recovers from her gyrating position, and to the painful but embarrassing tune of jeering shouts, she half-retrieves the paraphernalia. The trio rush out in single file amid bouts of boos, insults and heckle.

Meanwhile Dumba and his lawyer, Mr Thakor, hold a mini-conference in the car. They go over the salient points of the case so far. Unruffled, they go through the possible strategies to take now that the worse has come to the worst. They chart the next course of action regarding mitigation. What should now be avoided is incarceration. The priorities should be a wholly suspended sentence, a fine or release on bail pending an appeal to the Supreme Court.

*   *   *   *

It is exactly one week after the day of misjudgement. Dr Dumba is at home having dinner with Una, children and his two brothers. At about seven o'clock the phone rings. It is Mr Thakor, in hospital. He politely asks Dr Dumba to come over to the privately run hospital first thing in the morning. There is some very urgent matter to discuss concerning the case vis-a-vis his own health.

In spite of the persistent and worried questioning from Dumba, Thakor does not give further details. He hangs up. Dumba goes back to the table where everyone looks into his worried face. Could it be that Thakor has been involved in an accident. Why should he phone from the hospital. The intensive care unit of the hospital for that matter. Why meet at the hospital and not at his office or home as usual. The answers to these questions have to wait until morning. Some issues resolve themselves with time. Time is the biggest solver of issues.

Dumba finds Thakor sitting in bed in a characteristic pose, his knees up, a yellow pad on his lap. A reading lamp throws a thin beam on him; the rest of the room is in shadows broken only by the lights from the hospital grounds. Dumba's fears are confirmed. The worst has happened. Whatever it is it has necessitated the premature end of their perfect legal relationship.

Concisely Thakor informs Dumba that he has suffered a mild cardiac arrest. This will incapacitate him for weeks, may be months. He suggests Dumba be represented by a young upcoming African lawyer who has just opened his own practice in town. He should be able to handle rather competently the remaining simple task of mitigating. Thakor has arranged that a leading advocate be instructed by a firm of lawyers in the capital to represent Dumba at the Supreme court when the case goes up for appeal.

Dumba and Thakor agree, that whatever the outcome on the day of sentence, they are to appeal against both conviction and sentence. He assures Dumba that justice would be done, and seen to be

30

done, at least at the Supreme Court. He would be vindicated by the professional lawyers who sit on the bench at the highest court. The natural law of justice would see him free.

The next day Dumba goes to see the new lawyer. He is in his early, thirties. He looks and sounds average, more on the mediocre side. The sharp and perceptive Dumba is not impressed. Dumba notices that he lacks the sharp, inquisitive, cunning and aggressive qualities of Mr Thakor. It is too late for Dumba to change and scout around for a better lawyer with experience in cases of this nature. He resignedly decides to give him a try.

Back home, Dumba shares his anxieties with Una, who gives him some encouragement by suggesting that sometimes still waters run very deep. The new lawyer should be given the benefit of the doubt. Who knows, Una speculates, some people are capable of springing surprises.

In some way she is right. Two days before the continuation of the trial the lawyer surprises Dumba by twice forgetting appointments with his client. When they finally meet he keeps on mixing up names and cases, divorce cases included. Dumba gets really disenchanted but there is little he can do at this late hour. He leaves everything to chance, luck and fate. The gods are known to rescue the innocent even from the jaws of lions. Who knows, Dumba recalls Una's advice, the new lawyer, with luck, might spring positive surprises.

The day for mitigation and sentence falls on Thursday August 10. Dumba, Una and the children have their breakfast together as usual, though early. Una decides to make it an elaborate affair as if it is their last breakfast together for a long time to come. They all enjoy it though rather solemnly. Una cheers her husband up with jokes and anecdotes.

She is indirectly reassuring her husband that all will be well. All will not be lost. Things should be all right. No sane magistrate is so unreasonable as to incarcerate an innocent person, let alone a highly qualified person whose services would be sorely missed by the nation. It would be criminal insanity. It would be treasonable.

The court, like most third rate courts in this part of the world, sits six hours after its scheduled time. The new defence lawyer works on his mitigation. He tells the court that Dr Dumba is a very highly qualified person with four degrees in very specialised areas.

'His expertise, skills and knowledge are crucial to the development of this young country. He is a family man with wife and children. Furthermore, there is no prejudice in this case since the company's books are balancing. They have their money. No evidence has been led on at least four counts of the case. There are so many inconsistencies and irregularities that the accused should have been given more than the benefit of the doubt.'

The lawyer further pleads with the court to take all the fifteen counts as one for sentence since Dumba is a first offender. He asks the court to give Dumba a wholly suspended sentence, failing which it should impose a fine. 'Stone walls do not a prison make. The nation, society, the family and the person do not benefit at all from his incarceration. In fact, they all stand to lose considerably. It is a futile, destructive exercise.'

The acting prosecutor in turn rises to speak. He accedes to the fact that Dumba is highly qualified. However, he feels the court should take a serious view of the offence. A custodial sentence would act as a deterrent.

The magistrate adjourns the proceedings for ten minutes to consider the submissions.

The ten minutes become thirty. Eventually the magistrate, Mugo, resumes his seat. He follows the sentencing ritual parrot-like. He, ostensibly, promises to take into consideration everything the defence counsel has said when passing sentence. However, he takes a serious view of the offence so the courts must impose stiff sentences. He announces.

'A custody sentence is called for in the interests of society. So I sentences Dumba to 36 months, 7 days and 2 hours with labour. Nine months bare suspended on condition Dumba does not commit a similar offence. A further 9 months is suspended on condition he pays restitution of $10 000 by December this year. So Dumba will serve an effective sentence of 18 months, 7 days and 2 hours.'

The defence counsel rises to announce that he is to appeal against both conviction and sentence.

'The sentence is both shocking and excessive. It is unwarranted. So he is applying for bail pending appeal.'

Mugo flatly refuses Dumba bail pending appeal since he feels there is little chance of the appeal succeeding. He concludes in his strange English.

'In the interests of injustice, sorry injustice, and the accused she must start serving now, now. She must be deprived of his wife's warmth, sorry his bed. He must not continue to enjoy the bed, you see!'

The sentence is given callously, vindictively and arbitrarily to a mortal by a mere fellow mortal cast in a false mould of infallibility. A single stroke of a pen from a slovenly trained justice seals the fate of a person.

The absurd power of a whim to decide a person's fate. Does one have the duty to be harsh, to be cruel? Partiality is in itself an act of injustice.

People like this magistrate, Mugo do not shrink from using the cruel butt of their judicial rifles on the innocent. This is mercenary justice. These are justices of fortune.

But the truth remains. The ghost of their injustice will definitely reappear over and over to haunt them to their graves. Injustice, like the recalcitrant unappeased spirit of the callously murdered victim, will continue to rear its angry head, wreaking havoc on the lives and consciences of its perpetrators and their offspring. Any way and for now, Mugo's cruel, unkind, unfeeling and unconcerned statement seals the fate but not the future of Dumba.

An old wisened man in the crowd asks aloud the basis of the outrageous amount for restitution given.

' Is it a ransom to be paid before Dumba's release. Does failure to pay mean the hostage prisoner is simply livestock to be kept alive until brought to the market, or slaughter. What a cruel, unfeeling set up.' the wise old man asserts: we cannot honestly sit in judgement; being human, we too are probably wrong, more evil, only that the selective and arbitrary searchlight of the law has not fallen on us. He who judges knows how he himself will be judged!

As Dumba is led away by two prison warders, a man in his mid fifties questions aloud why unfair things happen to good people. "That man, 'he pronounces his prophecy, 'being led away is going to be a great man! This is a preparation for grater things to him. God has a noble purpose for allowing such injustice to take place. His ancestral spirits are with. All of you remember Jesus' trial before Pontius Pilate? It had a purpose didn't it?

'Let me tell you one thing. You can never stop the rising sun. This man will rise and shine! All of you, including the afflicting magistrate, mark my words! I never speak in vain. My words always come true!'

Una watches solemnly but bravely as her husband is led away. She has been watching the unfair trial, the farce with a deep sense of doom but not despair. The prayer that has eluded her all along comes to her: that fate would be kind to this good man, that his heart would be stout and that God and the ancestral spirits would keep his safe. She remembers the best of times they have had together. Now enter the worst of times. She hears herself soliloquize.

'We have had so much of happiness, of love, of fun and laughter. And I have not had enough; I want more, years and years of tomorrows. But not alone; never alone without that man. I will not! Hold it...wait...I want to tell this man how much I love him. I love him more than anything, more than life. Why is it that I can never think of the right thing to say at the right time? There he is my life, my love, just looking at me. I will tell him I love him. Look, there is no self-pity in his face. There is peace in him. And he wants to share it with me.'

'We have quarrelled and learnt how to forgive. We have faced the unknown together. He has shown me, taught me, shared with me and he has not changed. He gives me strength; courage is coming back into me. It is strange that I feel all these things all at once- love, fear, wonder, admiration and pride.'

'It is really strange. Here we are, still together, and yet so far apart, separated by the enemy of our love, of our compassion, of our progress. We will defeat the enemy, banish him from our lives. We will again be together; and be happy ever after. I know my husband well. He has a third eye for those things that make a person survive. I know that his dominant quality is calmness. It is one of the things that make him good at his job, a good husband and father. I know he would expect it in me now.'

'Anyway, everything in life has its price, and good things cost more than bad things. It is a known secret of life that victory over odds comes to the brave. Fortune favours the bold. So for his sake, for the sake of the children and mine I must remain calm and face problems, in fact the world, with courage, fortitude and determination.'

*   *   *   *

The evening sees victory celebrations at Zariri's place. The party is attended by all conspirators. The spirit of hatred is abroad with the success of *ODE*. Mr Igneous Mugo steals the lime light as he recounts the day's events at the court. He is a hero. As they crowd round the speaker Zariri has changed her seat for one where she could obtain a better view of the scene. She keeps giggling to herself, and surreptitiously digging chief Makope in the ribs each time Dumba's name is mentioned. Makope on his part can hardly conceal his joy at having finally dealt Dumba the last blow.

The party warms up to the bizarre sounds of the ox-hide drum, the thumb piano, the duiker horn, the calabash rattles, the whistles and ululations. The house vibrates, and the atmosphere fills with the eerie cosmic echoes.

Zariri dances in an attitude of complete abandon, her enormous hips grinding in a provocative imitation of the sexual act. Makope on his part performs an exuberant jig of delight. They leap for joy, hug each other grinning from ear to ear. The singing, the nerve-rattling vibrations, the stamping feet, the groans and moans, the chants, the cheers, the shrill ululations last into the small hours of the morning.

It is a spectacle of an incredible, unhappy and illogical system only found in the so-called Third World. Imposed mediocrities, like Trial Makope, as leaders do more damage than the plague because the mediocrity, if he thinks at all, always thinks that there are better people out there scheming to overthrow him and take his place.

Since he fears even his own shadow, he must destroy all those who could overshadow him. Successful and competent people like Dumba overshadow the people on top. People like Dumba break the cardinal rule in the kingdom of the mediocre: there shall be no other hero save the boss. Small wonder the logic of mediocrity turns the brain drain away from the devastated wastelands of Africa to the greener pastures of the developed countries.

In Africa incompetence and loyalty are the key to survival. In this part of the world common sense often dictates that the pursuit of truth is not always the wisest thing to do. And the handful of brave souls who do so do it at their own peril, literally. For they, almost invariably, are made to give up the ghost. Because of this the African scholar can be pardoned for what is increasingly becoming apparent as a deliberate evasion of truth or objective discussion. The tendency to swim and go along with the popular tide of fantasising as well as glorifying about Africans and glossing over their mistakes is very tempting. In the process it makes sycophancy a daily practice, because of the need to survive tyranny and intimidation.

Totalitarianism reigns supreme on the African continent but we do not run short of reasons to justify it. Because of the prejudices and inaccuracies, and because we strive so hard to find scapegoats for our failures, we cannot be sincere. It seems nowadays Africans find nothing wrong in keeping silent when Africans massacre their fellow people. The deafening silence sounds as though by some miracle the massacred would come back to life.

There is even a strong school of thought gaining currency that Africans are incapable of a democratic form of government. In other words, in our efforts to justify ourselves we are in the process of denying our very humanity. Our failure to admit our own humanity, and therefore our mistakes, makes us incapable of dealing with those mistakes. This can only earn us international scorn and contempt.

To add to the woes and misery of Africa, the continent is not short of those extraordinary creatures that evolution sometimes throws up. They are the African proverbial witching owls who stare at their victims with holes for eyes that seem to reach down into hell itself. They are a disaster for the human race. One wonders how it happens that such monsters are allowed to control the destinies of millions of people.

All this is what people like Dumba stand up to fight. They suffer for it. And they struggle against it. But for Dumba and the like there are many victories worse than a defeat. After all, life goes on after a nightmare, or even a dream, has ended. For they shall rise to defeat injustice, tyranny and oppression.

Six

THE INTERNMENT

Dumba is bundled into an over-crowded prison van chained to another weary-looking man. They sit on and collide with one another as the van speeds hazardously towards a prison complex forty kilometres east of town. The human cargo is tossed up and about as the driver negotiates the tortuous, bumpy and corrugated road. The occupants hardly exchange words save to gasp at the suicidal and murderous speed.

And so the journey continues as the van lurches and shudders on the road. The driver puts his heavy foot down on the accelerator as if speed is the object of the journey rather than the destination. The driver, wedged between the angle of the door and the seat, could hardly be bothered to glance at the road ahead. Frequently, he would remove his hands from the steering wheel to emphasise some point to the fat man sitting next to him and with whom he is in deep conversation.

The driver is a wild looking man with the guts of a cave man. His fierceness is exaggerated by his cheeks that are deeply scored by ethnic ritual scarring. He is some form of monster.

The condition of his vehicle worsens the situation. It does not instil any sense of safety at all. The vehicle is as battered within as it is without. The door does not close properly. The windows cannot be rolled down because the levers are broken. The stuffing is coming out of the seats. The uncarpeted floor, sticky with grease and dust, looks as if it has been sprayed by a burst of machine gun fire. The needle of the speedometer is missing.

As they are about to reach their destination some ominous noises start up in the engine. These horrible noises are followed by more frightening eruptions of smoke. Everyone inside, except the driver, chokes with smoke. Perhaps the driver's system is used to the frequent eruptions of smoke. For those not used to the smog it is suffocating.

The engine seems to be missing and back-firing. The pop, pop, popping of the back-firing engine scares the animals grazing near the road. They stampede towards safety. The battered vehicle has clearly, and audibly, seen better days. Then the over-used and abused wagon gives a mechanical gasp followed by a gallant but defiant back-fire and the engine goes quiet.

The warders and the driver get out and stand around the vehicle helplessly. After looking at it for some time as if a miracle is to happen, the driver lifts the bonnet. He commences tinkering with the engine, while the others look on. Occasionally, the driver calls to one of the warders to try the starter, but other than it making an unhealthy tired grinding noise, the engine does not fire. The driver pushes, pulls and prods everything vaguely mechanical that can be pushed, pulled and prodded without making any difference to the sleeping engine.

Someone suggests a push may do the trick. So the driver gets behind the wheel and the warders push. They push, and push...and push the fully prisoner-loaded vehicle until suddenly, and totally unexpectedly, the engine splutters into life. The exhausted pushers clamber gratefully aboard panting and gasping.

They reach the prison complex that sprawls over a large area. It is deliberately tucked away from society and the public eye. It is an eye sore. The prison farm covers a big area, close on 500 hectares. It combines prison facilities with forced labour camp conditions, Dumba learns from his fellow chain mate.

They scramble out of the van and are rudely headed towards an open space. A prisoner throws crumpled prison garb, of shorts and shirt, at each one of them.

A jailer approaches them with hands akimbo. His face seems to have been planned by an adhoc committee. He wears a crumpled face - loony, serene and disgusted all at once - with liquid eyes that shine. His eye lashes are as long as a cover girl's. The large nostrils take up a fifth of his face. The nostrils can close against blowing sand. One can almost swing on his bad breath.

He is a small creature who loves to harangue prisoners. He barks incomprehensible orders at the new prisoners. The man-like-animal shouts in a beastly voice of thunder. The bleating guard opens and shuts his big beak of a mouth as though it is on hinges.

Dumba and company are made to strip bare in the open verandah. As they are paraded nude one by one infront of the jeering jailers they are given a prison number to be learnt by heart. The prisoners hurriedly put on the prison garb and their own clothes are stuffed into separate numbered sacks. They wear no underpants and walk barefoot.

Surprisingly even in the loose prison garb, Dumba remains proud and dignified. But for his chain mate it is too much. The man begins to sob and talk to himself. It is a shock. The prisoners are headed towards a room where they are each handed a bedroll, three thread bare blankets, a collapsed aluminium cup, a battered aluminium bowl and half a piece of what was a towel.

They are shepherded into the jail section with holding cells built in a half shaped rectangle with open space infront and in the middle. The open space is all soil and sand. In the centre is a conspicuous humped rock. A big bare shed sits incongruously in one corner.

Word of Dumba's trial, conviction and arrival has already reached the prison camp of 900 inmates. A crowd curiously gathers to greet him. They ask him about current affairs 'outside', whether there is any news of an impending amnesty for prisoners. The inmates know and love the smell of news.

In return they inform Dumba of the appalling conditions in prison. The food here would not be eaten by animals. The meat, when meat is available, is but pieces of lungs and sex organs. The food is always terrible and the same, day in day out. The jailers say prisoners, like the starving, eat anything. There are no special arrangements; you have to eat whatever is available. Yes brother, whatever is available and is given to every prisoner is given to you.

Breakfast is a cup of dark coloured liquid and a squashed slice of bread smeared on the outside with some foul tasting syrup. It looks and tastes like pig's shit. You are forced to close your eyes to eat it. Amidst shouts and name-calling such as 'bandit, idiot' the prisoners are made to crouch and crawl for their food in rain or scorching sun. Mate, prisoners are treated like animals.

The litany of horrors shifts to appalling sleeping conditions for the prisoners. The cells are over crowded. They sleep on edge, knitted and so close together that they have to turn, on a signal, as one twice a night. Their bedding is a nightmare. There is more lice and nits than thread on the blankets. Because of the heavy infestation of the lice the blankets vibrate and quiver with the rhythmic movement of a slow moving snake.

Harrowing tales of ill treatment pour out. The work on the prison farm is slavery. The jailers are slave-drivers. They are cruel *mahoot*. They are insulting and persecuting. Prisoners are a source of cheap and free labour. You are driven to work by guards, whips, guns and vicious dogs until your every muscle aches; your every limb protests; until you are dog-tired and bone weary. Prisoners are made to work with a relentless rhythm in a state of perpetual motion tormented by guards always on the prowl with vicious whips and dogs. He who dares to pause for a breath or to rest a muscle is set upon, first by a guard dog trained to mount the offending inmate in imitation of the sexual act. Then the guards would descend on the poor bastard with whips, boots, fists, teeth and spittle. On occasion, favoured prisoners called 'staff are made to attack their fellow inmates in the standard fashion. The prisoners are kept hard at work till sunset.

To save fuel, inmates are made to pull the plough, to draw the cart, and at harvest time, to carry 100kg bags of grain two kilometres from the fields to the storage points. Brother, people who do not believe in hell have never tried to get inside an African prison. This place is real hell on earth, on African soil presided over by devils. It is hard to appreciate the full horror of life in these prison camps. If there is any heritage from the European colonisers to the African ruler it is the prison system.

As if to underscore the horror of the place Dumba's attention is drawn to a figure in the distance slowly making its way towards where they are standing. The figure is leaning far forward, dangerously off-balance, taking small, rapid, shuffling steps. The figure comes close and turns into a young man of about twenty. He performs a curious involuntary increase in the speed of walking, apparently in an effort to catch up with a displaced centre of gravity. He never quite catches up though he tries hard with mouth twisted in a soundless cry.

Before Dumba could ask what is the matter with the young man, a rather imposing respectable gentleman nearby displays an abnormal motor activity. He constantly shifts his weight from leg to leg and his pelvis rotates slightly. This is not unlike the bumps and grinds of strip-tease performers. It is startling to see them being done by this aristocratic gentleman.

Enquiries reveal that the two men had sustained injury to body and limb at the hands of the state interrogators. The central nervous system has been severely damaged, perhaps for life. Tampering with their victims' body, limb, and not infrequently life, is standard practice by law enforcement agencies.

The horrendous practice is sanctioned by the authorities up to the president. On one of the president's many visits to police holding cells he is reported to have demonstrated the skills of torture himself on an innocent looking suspect. He used a hot poker on the poor fellow without any remorse. In fact the president seemed to enjoy it. It is not surprising; the fellow has a lot of blood on his hands.

So small wonder the police, the law enforcement agencies use it religiously and zealously on victims who happen to be in their custody. The legacy is left in perforated eardrums as a quarter of the prison population is hard of hearing or suffer from septic ears; they turn round to tune in with the right ear when spoken to. Men with hanging balls, resembling those of old kangaroos, wobble around, as a result of heavy weights having been suspended on them by law enforcement interrogators.

As a pathetic encore two young men go past Dumba in style - a form of rock'n'roll cum *chachacha* step. The hula-dancing figures slowly disappear into the distance. What a sad real life zoo and circus rolled into one. This one very pathetic, Dumba muses.

*   *   *   *

Supper is at 3.00pm. Dumba finds the food tasteless and uneatable. Fellow prisoners, rather fellow sufferers, are more human than the jailers. Seeing the situation they start bringing their treasured smuggled bread and fruits to Dumba. A tremendous feeling arises in him. He is touched, really touched by such generosity and selflessness. Seldom in one's journey through life is one privileged to meet truly wonderful human beings.

After supper, more fellow sufferers exchange their relatively newer blankets for Dumba's tattered rags. A middle aged man donates his only humble but indispensable pair of sandals to the bare-footed brother. The inmates try by all means to make their new colleague, a comrade-in-agony, feel at home. A home of dehumanising brutality.

Bed time is at 4.30pm. After being counted in rows of five and recounted in rows of two they are locked up for the night and left to their own devices. They are twenty five in the cell.

Each inmate is introduced to Dumba by the cell chairman. They call him cell staff. Dumba quickly learns that there are businessmen, former civil servants who fell foul of their bosses, accountants and other professionals among the inmates. Most of them are weary of the long imprisonment. The rules of the habitation of the cell are recapitulated for the benefit of the new-comer as well as the old members.

A small but precious heart-warming welcoming party is held punctuated with song, short speeches, applause, smuggled tea and biscuits. As Dumba joins these quiet, worshipful folk in song, he begins to think that this modest, simple ceremony by these modest but not simple people captures the real true meaning of life.

The occasion is closed with a short but moving prayer soliciting, imploring God and the Ancestral Spirits to intervene in softening the hearts of the authorities, and to give them wisdom and the courage to forgive, forget and understand that after all is said and done we are all human.

At 8.00pm the lights are switched off. Another short prayer comes from an inmate nicknamed Comrade Reverend. He briefly asks God the almighty, the Ancestral Spirits, and the Great Spirit at the most holy shrine to remind the selfish unfeeling authorities: that they themselves are human, mortal and fallible beings. Hence they should forgive others. End of prayer. The inmates show their approval and appreciation with a lively chorus of *amen*. After a lapse of time all is quiet.

However, Dumba finds it very difficult to go to sleep in such an uncomfortable environment. For a start he has a man's knee in his face. Another unknown bedfellow swings his legs across Dumba's vulnerable belly. Another man talks loudly in his sleep. A man in the corner suddenly sits up and begins singing, then falls back into slumber. Yet another man somewhere in the room claps hands, crosses his arms in mysterious gestures; intones some ancient chants that nobody understands. One snoring male sounds like a chain saw, another like a steam engine. And another gurgles like a choking frog. Yet another like a growling hyena. It is an unco-ordinated symphony, rather a cacophony of snores.

Finally sleep comes to Dumba. But somehow he is shaken awake but slowly. As he slowly opens his eyes people in dark overalls dart to and fro and around the room. Gradually he realises it is naked inmates taking advantage of cover of darkness to relieve themselves at the hole in the centre of the cell that serves as a toilet.

Now sleep stubbornly refuses to come to Dumba. He spends hours gazing at the roof of the cell. Solitude can be rewarding. It can be created in the mind where ever a person can spend time alone, even in the overcrowded cell. He recovers both the appetite for being alone and its fruitful products: self-awareness and thinking.

Challenges make one discover things about oneself that one never really knew. They are what make the instrument stretch - what make one go beyond the norm. No amount of trouble could conquer him. Against apparently insurmountable odds he faces the world with wit and courage.

He knows without a shadow of doubt that he is indestructible. He reminds himself of the fact that of all the people he will know in a life time, he is the only one he will never leave nor lose.

To the question of his life, he is the only answer. To the problems of his life, he is the only solution. He must learn to live and love all the things that make storms in life -controversy, criticism, reverses; loss of freedom, of loved ones, of the precious things of life. He must not depend on another person for courage; or expect to hitch a free ride on another person's strength. You are your own best friend. Learn to hug yourself man.

The other person -a loved one, a dear parent, a caring friend, a caregiver -stands by with skills and compassion but they are limited. They shine a light into the dark tunnel of life but he must walk it alone. He was born alone. He came into this world alone. He will leave it alone. These are the true facts of life. There is no doubt about that. Life, misfortune, like death, like fate, conies to one individually. It is a personal experience, a personal visitation...one that cannot be shared.

Dumba's thoughts bring to his lonely mind more light than heat. He realises that although everything has changed, although wise people say the only constant is change, there is something that would outlast change. And that something is hope, not for a specific, not for a certain way or means, but hope that is very deep, very basic but very private within us all.

Because of hope those who suffer are more likely to make important contributions to the world than those who merely drift luke warm through life. The flawed person frequently has greater drive, greater ambition, hence greater need for success. The flawed person has great opportunities for growth, for improvement, for work. And who, after all, is not flawed. To have flaws is but human. Who is infallible? Who is superhuman?

Inspiration and success, like hope, come from seemingly contradictory sources. On reflection Dumba realises that he owes much to his friends; but all things considered, it strikes him that he owes even more to his enemies. The real person springs to life under a sting even better than under a caress. He, like the famous writer Andre

Gide, has enormous faith in the resilience of human beings, and of natural systems. Indeed he takes great pleasure in watching people and places rebound after a disaster.

He has never stopped being impressed in particular by the ability of human beings and of whole civilisations to change the course of their social trends; to start on new ventures, and often to take advantage of apparently hopeless situations for developing entirely novel formulas of life. So it is natural and noble to wrestle with all odds until final victory. For victory is certain to the determined, the valiant.

Dumba realises that he takes after his university professor who is an incurable optimist with a sweet, sentimental attachment to happy endings. Optimism is a creative philosophical attitude, because it encourages taking advantage of personal and social crises for the development of novel and more sensible ways of life. It makes one live, love and adore longer. It is the tonic to life.

Dumba has never been particularly religious, but at that moment he believes he sees the scheme of nature, the beauty and the horror, all fitting strangely into life's cycle.

Most people who are in jail go through stages similar to those of mourning for the death of a loved one: shock, emotional numbing, isolation and loneliness, sometimes serious depression, and impotence.

But for Dumba it is none of this. He is free even when he is in prison. His positive outlook, his thoughts, his dreams, his aspirations, his hopes cannot be physically destroyed. There is no change in his inner consciousness. Strangely he seems to be somehow fascinated by the whole scenario. It is a great learning experience. He fears nobody else except God. He is the centre of the cyclone. A tremendous feeling arises in him. Even if they throw him into hell, they cannot disturb his inner peace, his inner paradise. They may be bigger than he is, but they are smaller than life. Where ever he is, his peace, his paradise will be with him. They can kill him, but they cannot kill his spirit, his inner peace. He, like nature, is indestructible. There are certain things, certain people, they cannot destroy.

Dumba's thoughts come to a sudden stop. The inmates are roused by clangs of keys and yelling from the jailers. They quickly put on the prison garb, fold the blankets and roll up the bedrolls. In a flash they are all out and fall into lines of twos as the jailers, wielding batons, rattle 'fall into line bandits.'

The jailers are grim and frightening as that dread prison is unlocked. The jailers are in their usual ugly mood but not in their worst rages. When the latter happens their faces become horribly contorted, shrieking hysterically they reach an orgasm of sound and fury. Insults tumble out in a torrent as fists, booted feet and batons fly free style. They shout in a voice of thunder.

But thank goodness, this morning it is only the ugly mood abroad. Each inmate is told to listen and respond to the call out of his name and should respond with his prison number. After this ritual they are made to squat on their heels with tin mugs, spoons in their hands and lice in their shirts. Then they are made to crouch and crawl for their breakfast of 'tea and bread' amid jeering and insults from jailers standing over them. One rarely sees such humiliating scenes in sane society.

*   *   *   *

On day five of Dumba's imprisonment Una comes to visit her husband with the lawyer. She has struggled to get hold of the lawyer. She had to drive him in her own car from his offices to the prison. He says he could not come in time because of transport problems. His only car is out of order. Can you imagine a whole firm of lawyers with one solitary vehicle. So Una had no choice but to provide him with transport.

He brings, belatedly, Dumba the application for bail pending appeal documents for approval and signature. Una and Dumba are thoroughly disenchanted with the lawyer's lack of professionalism. His inefficiency is nauseating. The lawyer promises, rather unconvincingly, to speed up the very late application. So Dumba should hear from him within a week or two. What a charade? What a charlatan!

Seven

MEMOS OF LOVE AND SOLIDARITY

Most of Dumba's free time in prison is spent either receiving a stream of visitors or reading memos of solidarity from the family, colleagues, friends and well wishers. Dumba is happily surprised that so many many people care. All their messages are so full of encouragement, inspiration and warmth that Dumba is fascinated with this rare blend of humanity, wisdom, love, good humour and commonsense.

Dumba gets comfort from this card on solidarity from close colleagues. It says: *The people in your life are like the pillars on your verandah. Sometimes they hold you up, and sometimes they lean on you. Sometimes it is just enough to know they are standing by.* Another message is curt: *It's better to wear out than to rust out. Press on son of Dumba!* Yet another one advises him to rise and walk: *To fall is neither dangerous nor disgraceful, but to remain prostrate is both. You may be down but not out. Move on forward Dr Dumba.!* This one verges on adoration: *Admirers have long been hard pressed for fresh words of praise.* The loss of Dumba's services to his patients is akin to loss through death: *Blessed are those who mourn, for they shall be comforted. May these words of consolation somehow help to ease our sorrow and give you strength and courage for today and for tomorrow.* This one is more cheerful and optimistic: *Give the world the best you have and you'll get kicked in the teeth. Dumba continue to give the world the best you've got anyway.* Yet another one is prophetic: *Hope everything will soon be coming up rainbows. Happy days ahead!* The messages go on, and on.

Next in line of messages are those from his children. The youngsters' messages are more of graffiti yet perceptive and cute. *Dad: have another PhD degree in there. You know we are all on your side.* Another child has this to say: *My dad, make the worst, good out of it. Write a fantastic book out there. Cheers! See you soon.* Yet another one asks dad to read this: *A little white lie is a quivering, fragile flower which wilts when touched. Sooner than later, the truth will come out.* A longer message from the eldest child is entitled: The secret of true happiness. It goes: *Hello dad, this is just to remind you of what I read recently. It has a lot of significance. Here it is: Many intelligent people still equate happiness with fun. The truth is that fun and happiness have little or nothing in common. Fun is what we experience during an act. Happiness is what we experience after an act. It is a deeper more abiding emotion. You have to work for it. You have to suffer for it. The very true thing is that more times than not, things that lead to happiness involve some pain. And this present condition is indeed no exception. So we say, hang on in there and make good out of the worst. There is a saying that goes Do the right thing always. This may gratify some and astonish the rest. Dad be strong and count on us for support.* Together, the children end with the sentimental imperishable lyrics from Oscar Hammerstein's immortal song for Carousel called '

    'You'll Never Walk Alone,
        When you walk through a storm
        Hold your head up high
        And don't be afraid of the dark...'

Dumba is really moved. He is eternally grateful that he chose for a wife a cautious intelligent woman who gives him balance, and endows his children with a tenacity of will which enables the Dumba resilience, and brilliance to flower and prosper.

Una, on her part, is unusually brief most probably because of the agony she is in. She has taken her husband's place quite admirably. The life she has is tough. Dumba's mother shores her up and this gives her added strength. Women follow their own laws in life. They are great survivors. Perhaps the secret lies in their metabolic make up since they are the stronger sex biologically.

Her message is addressed sweetly to her love Henry. She heroically tells him that *you can do anything when you know you are not alone. So many, many people let us know they care: friends, relatives, former students and even strangers alike. You cannot know how wide and deep the goodness of people goes until you come up against an experience like this. You come to know who your real, true friend is.*

Mother and father are, as usual, pillars of support and anchors of hope. She finds the children sources of comfort, strength and consolation. They are just lovely and loving. My dear sweet Henry, life swings with the oscillations of a pendulum, sweet end, sour end, sweet end. Life is strange. What looks like disaster may turn out to be the best thing that happens to us. There is a blessing in disguise in this, our predicament.

For some, difficult times break relationships. But for us they solidify our bond of love. Difficult times are trying and can reveal real love for someone or fake love. I love you even more Henry. Together, let us revisit, sweet love, the immortal promise we made the day we married: 'in sickness and in health, for better or worse, until death us do part.' *I have the dream more than hope, the reality that very soon we will be together; and together we will stand, live and love. For my sake and for the sake of our beloved children smile away the troubles...keep on smiling darling Henry. You know Hove and care!*

Dumba is touched, moved, stunned, mesmerised, pained and uplifted by the heart-warming gestures of solidarity, care and love. It takes him time to fully recover from these emotions and to have the power to hazard a reply to his wife and children. He swallows his emotions and sits down to write to the children through his wife. He avoids being sentimental. He should remain academic, he tells himself. He should concentrate on the need to train the minds of the youngsters on strong will.

He thanks everyone for the excellent messages of love, hope and encouragement. He exhorts her to keep on the good work of raising strong, courageous and intelligent children. What greater gift can a parent leave to the child than the gift of courage. The heritage lies in giving the child a balanced diet of security and struggle. The child must have love, but not the surfeiting love that smothers self-reliance. The child must feel the whip and good of struggle, but not to the point where it is shattered by insecurity. This is the true art and science of being a good parent.

It is easy, my sweet dear Una, to be tragic about what a terrible world this is in which to bring up a child. That is nonsense. It is a fine time to have a child. It is merely a poor time to raise whiners, cry-babies and hiders-in-the-wardrobe. There are no absolutely safe places anymore. Softies had it easier in the past. There was a time when a person could live out all life and never witness a human crisis or hear a shot fired in anger. The modern child has no such assurance.

The road is in the hills and mountains now. It is along slippery and treacherous slopes. It clings to the precipices and looks down into the chasms. The distant vistas, of Canaan the promised land, are tremendously exciting. But it is no road for the frail-hearted and the timid. Durable are the children who have learnt to live and love the things that make storms in life - controversy, reverses, setbacks, criticism, misfortunes, challenges, problems, temporary defeats and tribulations. It is the world of the brave, the courageous, the strong-willed, the determined and the valiant. There is no easy way out.

Let me stop here my sweet love. Bye for now. Best regards to everyone.

Eight

THE SERMON ON THE ROCK

Sundays in this particular prison are ordinary, lazy but significant. Prisoners get up thirty minutes later than usual. After breakfast they assemble in the open centre of the prison complex. The small choir of ten inmates rehearses the three songs they are to sing during the service, one at the beginning, the second in the middle and the third at the end.

Prisoners look forward to this occasion for three main reasons. One, it is a day of rest and recreation, and perhaps recollection. Two, the prison chaplain, the Padre, is a very likeable, affable man who talks a lot of sense. Three, his sermons and speeches revolve on forgiveness and hopes of an early release for the inmates in the form of an amnesty. He provides and gives the yearned for morale booster. So he is held in high esteem by the inmates who regard him as their confidant and soul-giver.

Dumba's first Sunday in prison looks ordinary but becomes significant more for the Padre's powerful message than the beautiful, though at times out of key, singing. It is a moving experience.

The Padre arrives to thunderous applause. He takes his usual position on the humped rock. After the first song entitled *Silent Hope* the Padre asks the inmate Comrade Reverend to read a passage from the bible. The Psalmist laments

'My strength faileth me;
as for the light of mine eyes,
it also is gone from me...
I am ready to halt,
and my sorrow is continually before me.'

The Padre stands up on the humped rock. He tells his very attentive congregation that his theme is *Rise And Walk*. It has eight parts. He begins.

'We all understand the guilt and suffering experienced by the psalmist. Who among us can get through life without being struck down by trouble so great that we are ready to halt. Perhaps someone you love has left you or been snatched from you by death; or you have lost your job; or a beloved child is in trouble. Or you have done something wrong and are overburdened by the heavy load of guilt you are carrying.'

'The worst part of it is that when these personal crises come, we cannot imagine a way out. We are closed in, we feel. We may try various forms of running away - drugs, alcohol, meaningless love affairs, rounds of criminal activities. This kind of escapism is self-deceiving and self-defeating. This is contrary to our whole being that says we must strive to rise and walk again. Yes, the answer is that every cell in our bodies is programmed to fight for life.'

'Indeed life is not fair. To life, justice and fairness are non existent. They are illusions. Otherwise the bird would not feed on the worm, the hawk on the poor bird, the crocodile on the hawk and so on. We are here on earth to live, to experience whatever comes, to act on that experience as well as we can. That way we grow. My brothers, life is a candle meant to burn ever brighter, a fire meant to light other fires. It is a priceless gift from nature, from God, from our ancestors, and an inheritance for those who come after us.'

The Padre pauses for effect. He continues in his booming voice, his expression full of controlled emotion. 'My brothers, how do we learn to rise and walk? How do we learn to cherish life against the exhaustion of guilt or sorrow, or failure? How do we learn to hold on until the lights come on again? How do we come to that moment when even in our despair we say I can try again?'

'First, and foremost, invite yourself to live. Seek out those who have gone through the dark wood. You will find them all around you, every where, in life and in print. They are gallant people who are positive proof that life is worth living.'

'Second, forgive yourself, and others. Whatever the cause of our problems, we often see in it some real or imagined fault of our own. If we have done wrong, face it. Acknowledge the truth to yourself and God. With all your heart say you are sorry, you will not do it again. If there is restitution to be made, make it. We are never punished for our sins but by our sins. Then put your sins and failures behind you. And refill the pool of your life with new plans and enthusiasms.'

'But do not waste your valuable time and precious effort brooding over what others have done to you. Remember that people who hurt or hate you often do so out of their own problems, not out of their perception of you. No happy person hurts or hates. If you deserve the injury done to you, learn from it. If you do not deserve it, forget it by forgiving. That is the best medicine to life.'

Third, regain your self-esteem. Give up the defensive masks behind which most of us so often meet the world. Stand for your own values. Stand for your rights. Speak well of yourself, aloud and inwardly. Be as kind and generous to yourself as you would be to others.'

'You should stop expecting that you will fail. We often fail because we try for something bigger than ourselves. Think of what you have rather than what you lack. That is very important, for, in the depths of defeat, we often feel that we have nothing to give the world. So believe that you can bring to life some beauty, the shape and form of which you now can scarcely see.'

'Fourth, return to the world of other people. This is easier said than done. That may not be easy. We fear to face the world. We fear that the concern of others will renew our pain. And it is true that we do need time alone. But we must not stay too long on that lonely island in time, for in the end the way back to life is through our kinship with others.'

'For us to rise and walk again, we must love. Nothing more certainly wakes us from the life-denying apathy that follows disaster than love and care. Love and care force us to act. Find a compassionate person whom you can talk to from the bottom of your heart. Pour out all your woes and tribulations. You will feel not only refreshed but far better than staying in your own suffocating cacoon.'

The Padre pauses for a song from the choir. All join in the song *What A Friend We Have In Others*. He continues in his never-tiring voice...as before in colourful effective language. Dumba is impressed. He has rarely come across such an effective speaker. The man is really powerful. He is especially rich in the local language. Dumba's attention is again focused on the speaker who clears his voice. He exhorts

'Fifth, reach out to help. Help to others is the rent we have to pay for our room here on earth. My brothers, give your time and concern to others...thus in turn healing yourself. Helping others will certainly give you back your fresh lease of life.'

'Sixth, believe in miracles. Many people have experiences that seem to spring from a mysterious, ultimate self, bringing unexpected joy and strength. These people have seemingly come in contact with something larger than themselves, with a reality that transcends our world, a power that makes life pure and holy. This faith in rebirth, miraculous or born of our own struggles, gives us the conviction that we can grow beyond what is wrong with us.'

'In fact, the central message of the great crises in our lives is that we must be born again. So long as we are capable of self-renewal, we are living beings. So my brothers, welcome miracles. Expect to be born again not once but many times. Go where the mystery of life is closest to you -the pond, a chapel, a crowd of people. Listen to the voices within. Do not let your daily life be governed by trifling interests.'

'And my dear fellows, pray, meditate. Pray for miracles - an early release from trouble, from pain, from mental and physical torture, and from *prison'*. This part of the padre's speech is drowned in spontaneous applause. He patiently waits for a lull in the applause. And continues

'Please note that in all this prayer remains the great instrument of rebirth, of release from trouble, torture, prison, and of return to life.'

'Seventh, take one step at a time. Nobody can walk along two roads at the same time. If no miracles happen to you, settle for doing what comes next...for living one day at a time. Find ways to rise and walk. Cultivate and guard your own enthusiasms, however small they are. Respond to every small ray of hope that breaks into your dark world. Look for the little joys so usual and yet so sweet and cherishable. Look around you at the lovely, wonderful world of nature. Here another life is going on - flowers, trees, insects, birds, animals, people. Try watching one particular thing: the rainbow, the sounds of beautiful Africa, the angle of a bird's flight, the way the wind sways branches, twigs, leaves.'

'And finally, practise *pollyanna* power. Practise gratitude. Think of what you have that you do not deserve, and for which you should be prostrate with gratitude. For everything that goes wrong, there are probably ten or fifty or even a hundred blessings. Count them. A loving, dedicated and gallant spouse; lovely, wonderful children; understanding, forgiving parents; caring friends.'

'Everyday, especially when you are in trouble...when you are worried, look for reasons to be grateful. Thank God, nature, that the seasons come and go in endless variety. Be thankful for books, friends, the sound of music...and the way life forces us to rise and walk. My dear fellows, try such positive thinking and in time you will find yourself thanking nature, God, for making life as it is - the sorrow along with the joy. You may find yourself thinking - just to have been born, just to have lived at all - how wonderful that is.'

'My dear brothers, I repeat there are times when our failures, guilt and sorrows lead us to despair. But we need not give in. We should never, never despair. We should not give up! Never say die. Indeed, we can rise, walk again with our heads high, shine and live full happy lives. Problems, troubles, pain, tribulations, failures enrich our lives.'

The Padre receives a standing ovation, and the last but moving song: *God Loves Us All - The Good And The Bad.* With that the man, with a ready smile, and a great capacity, and appetite, for enjoying the simple sweet things of life, departs. Indeed, the Padre's sermons have spiritual voltage. What a powerful, wonderful speaker cum preacher.

Nine

A HAUNTED PLACE

Dumba finds prison a strange, abnormal and crazy world. What happens there belongs to the world of unreal reality. But what takes place over a space of a week borders on the supernatural.

The prison sits at the border of two cultures: the culture and science of normal society, and the sub-culture of an artificial person-made crowded environment. Many of its occupants, the jailers included, accept the idea of life at the edge of two worlds, this one and the next. The supernatural, the eerie world of spirits has the strongest influence on their psyche. Stories are told and retold of restless spirits. Believe them or not, the stories carry a thrill, a chill, a fascination that is overwhelming.

When these stories float around, Dumba dismisses them as a product of fertile imaginations, of troubled and bored minds. But what is to happen, some of it directly experienced by Dumba, is the story of a modern-day apparition. It does not haunt the dark corners of an old building or cave. It is seen and heard by average to above-average people. People of high intellect, in fact.

The building stands on the edge of a cell section of the prison complex. It is said to be the site of a bloody battle in the 19th century ethnic wars. When the foundations were being excavated skeletons of soldiers had been unearthed. To add to the spooky mystery two construction workers had fallen to their deaths as the building reached the roof level. A few years ago a jailer and two prisoners were found dead there for unkown reasons. This was within the perimeters of the fated building. Is one of them haunting the place? If a ghost is in the area whose spirit is it?

People at the prison camp believe ghosts are spirits of those who died suddenly, usually violently, and still have unfinished business in this world. They come back from time to time to carry on with their uncompleted chores. They periodically take rests depending on weather conditions, and disturbances near the site of their work.

It all starts on a Wednesday night. Two guards hear a crash in a back office. They look at each other. They listen. There it is again! The sound of footsteps moving slowly past. A door opens along the corridor. The guards exchange glances. Then a creak of a chair, as if someone has just sat down. The two guards search for the intruder. They look into every room. They are all empty. No sign of the intruder. The front and back doors are all locked.

But as they go back to their posts they see a shadow move past, go through a wall, and then come out again. They move with a start. There is what looks like a man standing in one of the walls. The guards narrow their eyes. For a few moments the man stays there before stepping into another wall. The darkness goes with him. Though without a shadow of his own, the dim light, where he is concerned, has lost its power. The guards blink and the man moves closer.

Both feel a cold hand that moves down their backs. Another crash. Without word, without any prompting, they flee, closing the door and turning the lock on the haunted place. They sprint fast and close, screaming on top of their lungs, past the cells with prisoners in the cells craning their necks to see what is the matter.

As they reach safety, light and others, their mates notice mud patches on the back of the panting guards' heads. Could it be the muddy heels of their own shoes touching their heads as they bent over backwards in a concerted effort to escape from the apparition? Or is it the work of the mischievous spirit engaging in some bizarre game?

As the story does its rounds the following morning Dumba is naturally sceptical. He is a well educated, level-headed person used to dealing with the hard facts and figures of the rational scientific world. Phenomena lose their awe as the search-light of scientific investigation falls on them. He knows that buildings creak, even fairly new ones like this one...sighing with the wind and groaning as walls expand and contract with changing temperatures.

Another problem area, Dumba reflects, is the human mind itself. An untrained, uninformed and unschooled mind can easily be fooled by natural phenomena. The job of the jailer does not demand the kind of a mind that has appetite for the scientific method. Perceptual illusion can make one see mirages, hear and visualise phantoms. As Marie Curie aptly stated, *nothing in life is to be feared nor taken for granted. It is only to be understood.* One can make a live venomous snake a belt...a lion a horse to ride with impunity and at leisure.

The following night promises uneventful. A new shift of guards is on duty. They are alert and wide awake...awake to the sound of even a pin dropping. Time passes. It is now close to midnight.

Suddenly, without warning, the guards feel the presence, as if somebody is approaching the place. For sure, there framed in the open doorway is a smoky, grey-black apparition. It is more than two metres tall. They can make out the oval of its head, the shape of the shoulders. Then it goes straight down...down. The guard blinks...but it is still there. He glimpses the face of his colleague, whose petrified look confirms the presence of the figure. When they look back at the doorway the apparition is gone.

The guards make a quick perfunctory search through the place but find nothing. But as they walk back up the corridor they feel a strange cold that lingers. They smell something musty like sulphur, a smell similar to that of a dead person. They hear the echo of footsteps behind them. They stop; so do the footsteps. They start walking again; so does someone else. They feel someone standing right behind them...only to turn around and find no one there.

The nearest wall seems to move...and then the inevitable cold hand runs down their backs...this time painfully slow...The crash. Oh no! They flee whistles blaring, and find safety in numbers.

They return in a group of other guards, the officer commanding bringing up the rear, armed to the teeth. Now nobody wants to be alone in the place. They methodically search the place high and low but find nothing. They decide to wait in one of the rooms in the building.

After a while one of the guards feels the seat of his chair begin to shake. The others try the chair, they feel the vibration too...a subtle but obvious movement that resembles the sexual act of a drunken but sleepy pair. Then the empty chair begins to move of its own accord. Good grief...oh no! The smell of fear spreads rapidly. The guards flee for dear life from the place en masse. And this time the officer commanding is leading the pack of the impromptu race, proving that he is Olympics material.

Once it is talked about the strange activities of the spirit increases. The mischievous spirit becomes strong and bold. Now nobody wants to work or guard the place at night. The authorities call in an electronics expert who goes over every bit of the building with a detector. He probes everywhere, even under the building's roof. He finds nothing untoward. Again the apparition is reported to visit the place at night undeterred by the electronic probing.

They try the services of the local medium to exorcise the evil spirit. The possessed woman describes the apparition as grey-black, and in ghost lore that means an evil wronged spirit...a spirit that can play practical and rude jokes on whoever happens to be in its area of operation. She confirms that the spirit has been there, in the place, for a long time. She sprinkles some herbs and burns some strong smelling powder...a mixture of hairs, snuff and marijuana. She chants, claps her hands and asks the spirit to vacate the place. She sneezes and bellows noisily as she marches out of the place.

After a few quiet nights the phantom continues to cause sleepless nights, proving that it has not vacated the place. A Catholic priest is asked to come and exorcise the place. As the priest prays for any lost souls wondering this part of the world he blesses room by room sprinkling it with *holy* water. At the last, and bigger room he draws back. What could it be? Is it propriety, deference, or has he too felt something? Has he sensed a sad presence, something not at peace with its environs, with itself, with others?

The power of suggestion can be awesome, Dumba confides to fellow inmates. All of it is in the mind. But what he knows is logical struggles in his mind with what he is now certain he has seen and heard. He continues to look for explanations.

For two days after the priest's visit there is calm. Perhaps it is out of spiritual respect...just as it has done with the lady medium. Or is it one of its tricks to appear to have been exorcised only to come back with a vengeance.

But late midnight, on the third day, Dumba and everyone see something misty trying to take shape at the door of the haunted place. They hear noises like someone picking up chairs and dropping them. They look closer and they see an office chair, that has not been there before, is framed in the door way. More chairs appear to array next to the first one. The spooky atmosphere fizzles out as a bright light suddenly flashes in the corridor. Then darkness follows. It is all quiet but eerie. Shadows carry sound with a deafening silence. The kind of silence one can chip away at with a chisel...the one you can hammer a nail into.

Word of the haunted place spreads. Offers of help arrive. A retired medical doctor wants to find out what the apparition seeks, and put it to rest. He resolves to spend a few nights at the place. The old doctor feels the phantom's presence, but when he is unable to get it to speak he becomes frustrated. He shouts at it to accept his help or go to hell. It does not like that. Immediately he feels a cold chill and terror that grip him long after he has left the place. A few days later he suffers a heart attack.

The apparition's final encounter is with the man with a ready smile, the Padre. He arrives at the place, says a prayer and stamps his feet forcefully on the floor. He explains that he is trying to crush the head of a serpent, a form that *Satan* sometimes takes.

As he turns to leave the place he feels some acute, stabbing pain in his foot. He takes off his shoe, then the stocking, to display two puncture marks on his heel. A snake bite! He announces the horror of the two fang marks to the astonished spectators.

Dumba is dumbfounded. He is visibly perplexed. The ways of the world are puzzling. Here are phenomena that need more than ordinary human intelligence to fathom. He has learnt one or two things in this place. Is there truly a phantom in this place? Is it a series of events that are connected by the human mind? Buildings do creak and groan. Sounds do carry in the night. Differences in light and darkness play tricks on the eyes. And shadows can become substance. The power of suggestion can be awesome.

Yet people, Dumba included, believe they have heard phantom sounds, have seen eerie sights, and have witnessed strange happenings. Indeed, some things have the habit of keeping their mystery. It is a strange, mysterious world that hides its secrets cleverly.

*   *   *   *

Yet another strange incident occurs on a Saturday afternoon. The Minister of Justice, Rehabilitation and Correction Services pays a rare visit to the prison complex. The ministerial party arrives in a fleet of black Mercedes, accompanied by their heavily armed bodyguards, all sporting aviator-type sunglasses. Their women are dressed in full-length imported prints, with the head of state's portrait strategically placed on their breasts, fronts and behinds. In this part of the world the head of state owns everything you see. The prints are of the wildest and most improbable colours.

Food, meat and alcoholic drink flow, and they are all now twittering and giggling like a flock of strange birds. The Minister of Justice's senior wife unbuttons her blouse, produces a succulent brown bosom, and gives the infant on her hip a late lunch while herself taking on copious quantities of clear liquor. She belches alcohol-laden smells that disturb the chickens scrounging around. As the mountains of food and drink disappear the officer commanding the prison stands up to introduce the dignitaries present. This is followed by political sloganeering ranging from praises for the head of state, the dear leader, to the blind, unwavering, unending, everlasting loyalty of the people to the leader and the ruling party. The political commercial ends with calls for death and destruction to those who dare oppose the leader and the ruling party.

The party winds up with a guided tour of the prison complex starting with the livestock section of the prison farm. As the ministerial entourage enters the bush surrounding the pens the call-away bird chirps excitedly. Unknown to them a leopard was resting in the boughs of a big fig tree under which the entourage has to pass in single file. The minister and his wives decide to take a path, a short cut, to the other side of the big sheep-pen. And in the process the big cat feels surrounded, and threatened. Its exit remains a narrow opening in the dense bush between the two parties.

The leopard is the most cunning and determined of all the dangerous game of Africa, except perhaps the buffalo. The leopard is possessed with lethal speed, tactical combat skills and strength. The lion will growl before charging and will fix its attention on one person. The elephant will turn under the punishment of heavy bullets in the chest. The buffalo may concentrate on one target at a time.

But the leopard comes in silence, going, with deadly accuracy, for those vital life points that immobilise the prey. When it comes to human beings, because of its experience with primates - baboons being its favourite food -the encounter is one sided almost all the time. The beast bounds from one person to the other with lightning speed maiming and killing in the process. It is known to destroy a party of professional hunters before they have a chance to fire a single shot. It goes instinctively for the head, taking off the sculp and top of the skull, while its back legs rip down the belly, stripping out the entrails with hooked sharp claws; all done with dazzling speed. Once it has charged only one thing will stop it - and that is death.

As the crowd closes in, chattering and jibbering excitedly, the leopard stands, listens and instinctively charts the likely path and pattern of approach. Human beings always spell danger for the leopard's dwindling population. It has been hunted and killed for pleasure, sport, skin and trophy. The hatred and anger begins to seethe in it.

Here the killing rage begins. It drops its head and lies flat on the bough of the fig tree, its body blending nicely with its natural surroundings. Its tail is the only part of its body that is moving. It uses it, like the witch doctor's fly switch, to divine its path of combat. It is acting on an atavistic memory: everything it does has been done countless times before by its ancestors. From listening, peering back, the gathering of tough muscle, the search for the ambuish point, it is all part of a pattern.

It is the minister's younger wife who by chance spots the tip of the moving tail and points it out to the minister who curiously goes to have a closer look. The leopard moves with deliberate stealth, insinuating its lithe body gently through the intertwined creeper and branch, a single pace at a time. Here it stops, hidden on the far edge of the tree, its body screened entirely by dense growth. The minister moves in still closer...blinks his eyes... and suddenly he looks into the eye itself - and it is like a glimpse into an inferno, the all consuming fire of the supernatural.

The beast leap-charges. The tree bursts open before the minister and his young wife, branches part, leaves shake and flutter as though struck by a whirlwind of brutal force. It comes fast, its jaws wide open with the front fangs flashing in the sun like a surgeon's scalpels. Tears of anger track wet lines down its hairy cheeks.

The honourable minister of justice carries the burden of flesh typical of those people in eating positions. He is least fleet-footed of the runners. His belly wobbles mountainously beneath his waistcoat. His face is as grey as last week's ashes, as he screams with terror and exhaustion. His bodyguards are leading everyone by a hundred paces and rapidly widening the gap.

The leopard lands a heavy blow with its paw on the minister's jaw catapulting him into the dust. A blow that would make the world boxing champions grow haggard with envy. Dust, and blood spurt from under him, enveloping man and beast.

Almost at the same time, and in the same instant, the leopard emerges from the cloud of dust as one of the younger ministerial wives sprints, shrilling with terror, across its path. It hooks at her with one forward-raked paw, and the points catch in the flying hem of her dress. But the young woman spins gymnastic style and the brightly coloured material unwraps from the woman's body like a loose towel.'

'She leaps into the air, lands awkwardly on one of the roofs of the sheep pens, catches her balance, and then...totally naked, goes bounding from one roof of the pen to the next with long legs flashing and abundant breasts bouncing elastically. Fear is the most potent drug. There is pandemonium. High officials overtake their wives, in a race for dear life. Infants strapped on the women's backs howl as loudly as their mothers.

The beast's attention seems to be distracted a moment by the gaudy dress caught in its paw. Now the panic stricken crowd has dispersed to a safe distance to watch the macabre scene, among them the still stark naked woman.

As the beast turns its avid attention to the honourable minister, its breathe, only a few centimeters from the ministerial backside, seems to physically revive and propel the minister as he turns out to be a much better climber than sprinter. He goes up the nearest mopani tree like an over fed squirrel, and hangs perilously in the lower branches with the beast coming up for him.

A dangerous cat and minister (mouse) game ensues with the beast tearing at the air with vicious swings of its razor-sharp tipped paws. Man and cat hop from branch to branch in a death dance. It glares at the cowering figure with murderous frustration.

However, with much practised feigned attacks it corners the minister and dives for his face, missing it by a hair's breath, but managing to catch hold of him by the beard. Both cat and man tumble to the ground and disappear in a cloud of dust. The crowd watches in fascinated horror as the now invisible game continues on the ground. The minister's senior wife involuntarily empties her bowels. She starts to raise her voice in keen mourning, a blood curdling, chilling sound of frightening proportions.

The bodyguards stand helpless as they cannot shoot with man and cat so entangled. At that moment a miracle happens. A short, skinny figure comes running towards the struggling bundle of cat and man. He wears prison garb of a discoloured type, the type that looks like a shroud...as if the person has just come out of a tomb. He imperiously moves close to where beast and man are locked in a one sided battle of strength with the ministerial and feline beards brushing.

'I greet you Great Spirit, the one who reigns the clouds!' He greets the leopard courteously clapping softly to show his profound respect.

The leopard swings its head to the sound of his voice and clearly sees him. It lets go the helpless, now still, minister and turns to face the man threateningly.

'Yes I bring good tidings to you, the most beautiful yet powerful fellow who has ever trodden this earth. We know you have come from the most exalted place!' The man advances two paces towards those vicious fangs and raised paw. He is still clapping his hands softly. The animal paws the air and makes a mock attack. The man stands his ground. There is a coldness in him where his own fear should be. Has he trained himself to that during the hard long bitter liberation war? What kind of person is he?

'Yes you have come to teach us a lesson in respect, honour and justice. You were not serious as you played games with us. It is a pity that this honourable minister and his harem do not appreciate your joke.' He gestures with his hands to the crowd that has now stopped fleeing. But he keeps his eyes on the animal. He continues to address the leopard

'Even this bunch of uncivilised bastards, whose mothers have slept with the dung-eating hyenas, have offended you by fleeing from a peace loving fellow like you.' The animal backs up a pace and performs another halfhearted mock charge. With deference, a reverence bordering on worshipping he concludes

'Big one, from the highest echelons of beyond I humbly, profusely apologise on behalf of this ununderstanding, unperceiving crowd here present and running the country, the continent and beyond. You have shown us clearly that death does not kill. Here the two of us stand alive yet we passed through death.'

The man stretches out his hand slowly, and they watch in breathless silence. At this point, the cat raises its paw, now the tallows are withdrawn, sheathed, resulting in a harmless, friendly fist of fur. The teddy fur you can cuddle and hug. The man steps forward as if to shake hands of peace with the animal...but there is commotion as the minister comes round and shouts for help at the top of his lungs. In the dust and commotion man and cat disappear leaving the tongue-tied crowd and the shocked and bruised minister raising a feeble little cheer of relief and disbelief.

A new commotion develops in the middle of the crowd. The minister's young wife is still stark naked. Someone rushes to cover her not so innocent nudity.

Ten

THE PRISON SCHOOL

It is now four weeks since Dumba's arrival at the prison. He has not heard from the lawyer inspite of repeated esquires to the lawyer verbally and in writing. Normally an application for bail pending appeal takes two days. But with the delays at the High Court it should take two weeks at most. It must be the inefficiency and incompetence of the lawyer, who shall remain nameless for his deeds are too shameful to warrant a name. Dumba decides to renounce agency and hire the services of a reputable firm of lawyers in the capital city.

After a week Dumba receives a letter from the new lawyers indicating inadequacies in the preparation and presentation of the application for bail pending appeal. They suggest that since it is now close on six weeks it is prudent to press on instead with the actual appeal against both conviction and sentence at the Supreme Court. They warn Dumba that it may take some time before the appeal is heard. It may take eight months. Even up there in the echelons of justice the wings of justice are about to flutter. Things have changed for worse.

It is disconcerting, frustrating and painful to wait that long in prison. At such a painfully slow pace, Dumba calculates, the appeal would be heard months after he has finished serving the unjust, unwarranted draconian sentence. These are the rough edges of third world justice where an innocent person is thrown into jail and forgotten. No one seems to care that delayed hearing is justice delayed...and justice delayed is justice denied. Unless one has a powerful friend or relative in the corridors of power one is destined to rot in prison. There are double standards in Third World-rate justice. In fact two kinds of justice: one for those in *eating* positions, and another for the poor and the powerless. These latter ones they call people of valueless opinions. In short *povo*.

Intellectuals like Dumba have no sympathy at all from the authorities since they are viewed as natural enemies of corruption and dictatorship. They easily see through the ruling elite's hypocrisy and double standards. They are victims of their own success. Their crime is bravery. They are persecuted because they are critical and competent.

In the gray and dismal realms of the third world politics they stand out and, therefore, have to be cut down. In the world of the mediocre, with the culture of mediocrity, the brilliant and outspoken is the enemy who must be destroyed so that blind persons can continue to be king. The principle guiding their kingdom is *if all fails just lower the standards!* It is the *chibuku* effect...dregs rising to the top. This is the world people like Dumba fight and struggle against.

No matter what...Dumba does not succumb to all these setbacks. He is more resilient than that, more spirited, intelligent and creative. The will to overcome hardships, the strength to live, emotionally as well as physically, is powerful and all there in Dumba. He is strengthened by adversity and even enriched by sadness. He reaches out to others by getting immersed in work on the fields, construction sites, the piggery and the chicken house.

Nevertheless, he is sickened, saddened and pained seeing inmates being kicked by jailers as if they are recalcitrant goats. They are hassled, starved and chased so much that their feet are not allowed to touch the ground. But in a sense the beatings are elating because they are defeating the jailers every time by resisting.

All the same Dumba presses on by involving himself in teaching literacy classes for the inmates. He also teaches language classes at all levels. His enthusiasm and involvement are so much that semi-formal classes are arranged. He recruits inmates with some 'O' level subjects to teach primary classes. He gives them crash courses and survival skills in teaching. Soon the interest in learning spreads to include a sizable number of jailers. The news of the learning movement reaches the prison authorities who, surprisingly, are impressed with the success that they transfer Dumba to an experimental prison school.

It is early summer when Dumba is moved to the prison school. One of summer's best fragrances is neither fruit nor flower. It is the sweet smell of rain when the drops come down and sink into the grateful, thirsty hot earth. Some of it land on to hot dry rock. It is the fragrance of peace as rain cools and soothes the heat of adversity.

The rain increases in intensity and velocity. It beats down in sharp, diagonal slashes, stinging Dumba's face. Dumba and the jailer accompanying him enter the three big prison gates as they open in quick succession. The gates suck and swallow the pair as a hungry chameleon does the butterfly.

Dumba finds this prison quite an improvement on the one he has just left. The guards are more of prison officers than punishers and jailers. They are more humane. Quite a number of the prison officers have had some professional training in trades and professions like nursing, teaching, carpentry, metalwork, agriculture. The rest are warders with a sprinkling of jailers proper.

The inmates are young averaging twenty five. Dumba finds the youngsters very friendly, likeable and soft-hearted. They are not hardened at all. They are eager to learn and to improve themselves. But the food and the sleeping conditions are just as appalling and primitive. The poorly cooked, prepared and served meals are there. The lice infected bedding and crowded cells exist. However, the inmates are treated comparatively better. They line up for their meals instead of crouching and crawling for it. *Teachers* have their own separate line.

*   *   *
*

Prison is the greatest education in life. No one can claim to be fully experienced without having gone through this traumatic life. If you have not been in prison, you have not lived! We all tend to think of prisoners as robbers, murderers, rapists, hard-boiled fellows. All terrible people. But in there you get to discover human beings in a way you never knew them before. You find that many of the so-called hard-boiled fellows have one thing in common. They are people of above average intelligence. Even those without the benefit of formal education.

If you have never been to prison, it may be perplexing that any normal, intelligent human being should want to commit crimes against society as such. Prison first teaches you that you have taken a lot for granted about life...about good and bad, justice and injustice, beauty and ugliness, virtue and vice. The word crime presupposes morality. Divorced from that morality, crime is an empty meaningless word. All through life one has been hearing nothing but the horror of crimes...the despicable character of criminals. But in prison for the first time, one learns that there is another side of the story. It is quite a revelation. Inside prison one finds out why crimes are committed. The real truth is never told in court, rarely in life.

Prison can be also quite an experience. Prison means taking orders from intellectual inferiors. It means being pushed around by power-mad eunuchs who have made a profession of locking up other people for reasons they themselves cannot understand. Prison means sharing one toilet with fifty strangers and bearing them watch you when it is your turn. It means standing in long queues for your morning shave...and sharing a *razor* blade with a dozen men. Prison means forced separation from loved ones. It means tolerating brutality dealt out by zombies in uniform, mother-f.....g fools with no shred of conscience at all.

Dumba is pleasantly surprised that even in prison among robbers, he ends by discovering human beings...real human beings. Unbelievable but true. There are here profound, strong, beautiful natures. And how joyous it is to find gold beneath that crust. How different it is from the heart of gold of officers of justice, of preachers, which is that of a hard-boiled egg!

*   *   *   *

Dumba is pleasantly surprised to find that lessons are properly timetabled for the morning and afternoon. But the learning hours are short and interruptions are common.

Still there are a number of disturbing, in fact alarming things Dumba notices. For example, a number of the prisoners are under age, below sixteen. Some of them are mere babies. He is shocked by the presence of youngsters with diminished responsibility who are in incarceration. Imbeciles, mentally retarded and unbalanced personalities, epileptics...are all there. These are people who should not be in prison at all in normal, civilised society.

For instance one young man spends most of his waking time gazing into space seeing nothing. Another one expends his energy chasing the wind. The youngsters are thrown into prison in all states of mind, shapes, sizes, ages and colours. The unjust justice system processes people and cases arbitrarily, machine-like or sausage-like. No one cares, no one has feelings. Prison is a refuse ground where societal rejects, the poor, the powerless, the sick, the unwanted and the deviant are all dumped with the forlorn hope against hope that they may reform by picking up one or two skills.

In this particular prison old prison cells have been turned into classrooms. Use is made of portable chalkboards. Classes range from adult literacy groups, primary grades, lower to middle and upper secondary levels. The number of inmates fluctuates but stabilises at three hundred plus or minus. The learners come from all parts of the country. It is the only school for prisoners who are twenty five or below.

Dumba has to work with twenty improvised *teachers* and only three qualified ones. Against this backdrop they have to mount a crash course for the unqualified teachers. On the credit side most of them are fairly effective teacher material, thanks to a judicious selection procedure. They quickly adopt and adapt the methods, the approaches and classroom survival skills. A fairly satisfactory professional group is forged out of them.

What surprises and impresses Dumba is the apparent lack of deviant antisocial behaviour exhibited by the inmates. Though their *crimes* range from rape, mostly statutory rape, car thefts, marijuana trafficking, poaching, fraud, theft, dealing in precious stones to insulting the president most of the young men seem quite normal. They are courteous, humorous, obedient, warm, considerate and very easy to work with. They are delightful to teach and befriend.

Dumba spends most of his time with them. On average he finds them pliant, very different from the incorrigible stereotype. One wonders why they are incarcerated. A wholly suspended sentence, or release on probation would have sufficed for most of them. They are over-punished. In fact they look so brutalised, so intimidated by the whole experience that they feel rejected and abandoned.

Like the insects entering a termite mound, they enter it and are never seen again for a very long time. These ravaged-looking persons in crumpled old clothes bear the marks of long privation. They live in intolerable discomfort. They are thin, ill, and ugly with suffering. What they need are not guards, barbed wire or high walls but homes, care, and affection. They need understanding, people with genuine feelings.

Alas, they show all the marks of physical and mental torture - perforated eardrums, septic inner ears, turning round to tune in with the better ear when spoken to, the now healed lacerations on the body...the strange gyrating movements: St' Vitas dance, the cock-eyed eyes, noses that are now many degrees out of true. It is a heart-renting sight that leaves you fighting a lump in your throat. All of it is the legacy of the law enforcement agents, who believe in the practice of riding rough-shod over the most basic of human rights.

Add to it the toll of victims from the excesses and abuses of the draconian provisions of the endemic state of emergency regulations prevailing in the country. So callous, so sadistic, so vindictive, so arbitrary the system is that it eats its own children in the name of maintaining law and order. It is horrifying and heart-breaking. Indeed, horror has a new home: prison.

Eleven

GRAINS OF SAND

Dumba is sitting watching all these miserable looking youngsters. Thoughts run through his mind. It is very strange and inhuman that only rational beings put other beings in cages like prison. For we know no other creature that is so barbaric and heartless as to pack its offspring, its future, into crates and cages to rot. What parent would sleep soundly when a generation of his or her children languish in concentration camps like these. These places are horrific...so terrible to live in.

Dumba mulls over this horrendous situation. Most of the time criminal justice is criminal. It commits crimes against humanity in the name of law and order.

African people are the most sufferers of hate and intolerance from fellow Africans especially those in power. It is still better to be *white* than *black* . We, Africans, lack the principles of love and tolerance. We have long lost these noble attributes. Hence we are unable to address injustice, poverty, degradation and suffering. We appear to lack a basic love for our people, and therefore, cannot make sacrifices on their behalf. This is in sharp contrast to the colonists who developed all and everything for the love of fellow whites.

We should love our people first in order to develop. There is no principle of love in our law, politics and economics. Without love in our law, politics and economics there can never be a happy country. Yet among those in positions of power today, either in the public or private sectors, is a frightening readiness to use force, imprisonment and dictatorial methods. The social and political costs for this anti-democracy will indeed be high. Our countries are full of talented people, and abound in great wealth and natural resources which can be fully developed if they are free. The rule of fair law is a miracle born of justice and fairness. It is nothing less than humanity protecting itself against its own cruelty and selfishness.

Patrick Wilmot's grieving words pierce Dumba's mind with the haunting sound of an African funeral horn.

There is something admirable and noble about the dog or cat which snarls, threatens and attacks when anyone or anything approaches its litter. There is something tragic about the maddened wailing of the wolf or fox howling for its young which is lost. After a while the dog, cat, wolf, fox no longer experiences the loss, or even the absence of the dead. Hormone levels adjust, as the programme for survival is reactivated as the reproductive capacity is restored. This is not surprising since the lower animals reproduce prolifically on the natural fact that only a small fraction of the young will survive.'

'But none of this compares with the gaze of a woman or man into the laughing cute eyes of a happy child. All this pales into insignificance with the empty gaze of the mother or father broken and distraught, as s/he holds the frail corpse of his or her young one in his or her arms.'

'In the human species the urge , the drive, the instinct to survive has been refined and transformed, we believe, through rationality and emotion...through the development of the intellect as well as the spirit and feelings. This has produced love and compassion.'

'Love is the greatest discovery in the evolution of human beings. Through love and compassion *homo -sapiens* made a quantum leap above other animals. This gave homo- sapiens a qualitative and decisive advantage in the struggle for survival and dominance. Love and compassion are the basis of human solidarity, fellow feeling, of the bonds which unite us as people.'

'Consider and imagine the mother or father, shattered by catastrophe of bereavement. Think of the grief which can continue to the end of one's life. The human being does not just lose, but is conscious, of this loss, is overwhelmed by it...or invents mythologies to justify and overcome it. The human being has not just an emotional bond with the child but reasons that the child is the future of the individual, the family, the line, the race, the society. A society that does not protect its own children, the youth, is a society without a future.'

The haunting Wilmot refrain yet again choruses with the sound of a pulsating burial drum.

'What then do we say of societies or individuals that sell their children into bondage, or allow them to starve, or be ravaged by disease...or worse put them into cages in the name of maintaining law and order. Let it not be said that it is because of a lack of resources. The resources have been sucked and squandered by the criminal, vampire elite who deposit the resources, plus the loans and grants in Western banks. Or they have bought, haven't they, expensive real estate, or expensive clothes...or posh cars, or expensive food and drink, or expensive harlots. They have invested them in private businesses. They have also acquired foreign tastes.'

'Where in the Third World, and Africa in particular, is any evidence of viable and productive projects on which these vast resources are expended? We do not see the evidence in schools or hospitals...or factories, or railways or other productive infrastructures. We fail to see it in housing or running water, or clinics, or electricity for the average person.'

'In remote African villages young mothers sit outside wretched huts, their precociously shrivelled breasts stuck in the gums of starving children. Their eyes are sunken, vacant, distant and without hope or consciousness. They do not know whether they themselves are alive or dead, and incapable of caring.'

'In the stagnant gutters of urban slums prematurely aged mothers void their wombs like vomit into the open pits. They cannot bear the agony of another empty mouth to feed. In other slums, villages, squatter camps, wards, streets and hamlets of a devastated continent other children die and are forgotten at the staggering rate of six million a year. Those who are lucky to survive face an uphill struggle as their bodies, their health, their lives are assaulted by poverty, corruption, cruelty and imprisonment.'

'They are forced to stay out of school, to scavenge, to steal, to prostitute themselves, to baby dump; to ravage their bodies with cheap alcohol and drugs. The dismal and horrifying statistics create the vast golgotha of Africa's permanent disaster areas. Disaster areas where their leaders who were once beggars take all and give nothing. One is deeply cut to the heart by such callousness. And God is there watching all this? May be God is in exile. We would ask him: *What have children to do with it?'*

'Meanwhile, the vampire elites, the beneficiaries of the resources, of the loans, of the grants, continue to grow fat. Their children go to school overseas, shop for toys at Hamleys. They buy their clothes at Harrods of London. The victims are punished while the real criminals not only go scot- free, but are shamelessly and spectacularly rewarded. Again Wilmot asks a pertinent rhetorical question: Who do you ask? Those who should answer are all dumb quiet with their mouths full of honey. He who keeps the company of the corrupt, even in silence, becomes corrupted.'

'As many of the children of the stinking slums and impoverished rural areas are packed into cages they find the same tragedy in prisons. Prison populations are rising at an alarming rate, no thanks to the unjust system, worsening economic conditions, extreme inequalities, crises of governance, corruption, repression and the litany of Africa's development problems. Almost all of them self-inflicted.'

The flame of hope flickers very low. At this rate it is not surprising that Africa, the once dark continent, is getting darker. The seemingly self-imposed holocaust is devastating. The big question is: Who can deliver the suffering trodden people, these grains of sand, these poor victims from the claws...the clutches of human-made poverty. The poor must continue to feed on hunger, to feed the crocodile or be eaten by it.

Dumba observes that each prison is a microcosm of the national and continental tragedy in neglect and human suffering: gross overcrowding, widespread disease, rampant malnourishment, minors in prison, harsh sentencing, long years of wrongful imprisonment, maltreatment of prisoners, and appalling conditions.

Even here, Dumba finds, a new slavery, and in the end he discovers he could no longer live without freedom, and in particular the freedom of his fellow people. He knows that he, alone, cannot redeem the world. But honestly is this to be the future of the next generation and the next? No, he has seen too much suffering, too much inhuman conditions that his heart bleeds.

But as usual he finds solace in involving himself with others.

*   *   *   *

Dumba decides to find out from the victims themselves, the inmates, what they think and feel of their intolerable condition both inside the prison and outside of it. What he is to discover and learn leaves him startled, fascinated, encouraged at the same time pained. He finds the young fellows quite articulate, perceptive and capable of using tools of analysis. They come forth in many forms: philosopher, politician, economist, humanitarian, lawyer, social critic, cynic, dramatist, cartoonist...and crook. It is a real fertile revolutionary seed bed of discontented, brutalised and bitter people. In fact it is a mirror reflection of their young counter parts outside prison though they themselves, for the moment, live in a world of unreal reality.

Dumba starts his research by asking a big-eared but sharp-eyed young man how he feels about life and present conditions. In a candid manner he answers

'If you belong to the wretched of the earth, the impoverished masses, and survive on hand to mouth scratchings like most of us, then you have to wait for the proverbial poetic justice to level things up. I remember the wretched of the earth out there: malnourished, starving, barefoot, potbellied, half-naked and miserable looking children, women, men made to line roads waving, dancing and cheering at VIP passengers in imported posh cars heading for their residences - heavens in hell. Women are made to kneel before these earthly gods.'

'I can clearly see the man, the chief, in a very expensive navy blue suit, thick gold-framed glasses, highly polished shoes with a solid gold Rolex watch, and an ornamental walking stick - his symbol of wisdom and power. The chief seems impervious to what the world think of him or his wealth...and the absolute poverty of his people, including his own villagers. He is not even ashamed to build a mansion, a palace, dwarfing his unfortunate villagers' rough grass huts.'

Another big-headed young fellow chips in.

These political leaders, the chiefs, are heartless. They live and swim in luxury: palaces, fat salaries, untaxed allowances. And they still want more. Their ill-gotten wealth stashed away in Swiss banks is almost double the country's national foreign debt. As if this day light robbery is not enough they build prestigious but white elephant structures. How many such other complexes do our African leaders have at the expense of the hungry, poor, unsheltered and sick masses? They travel in sleek luxurious Mecerdes Benz cars and multi-million private air planes while their nationals wallow in poverty. It is nauseating. It stinks up to hell. I believe our leaders have been hired by some invisible hand to destroy us.'

A usually sluggish and soft spoken young man springs to life. He sees red as he relates his experiences. He has read many stories and seen many documentaries on the impoverished, but actually seeing it is quite different. He tells Dumba that

'I grew up in an area that boasts an explosive reservoir of impoverished, unemployed and socio-politically frustrated youths all too willing to pick up a knife, a stone or a gun. So violent strife and crime are common in these areas. To survive they have to scrounge around, scratch for a living. They become creatures of Africa, where

the strong eat and the weak are eaten - or beaten, as the case may be.'
He pauses for breath and continues

It is strange that the consensus among the rich, those in feasting and eating positions, is that the poor are poor because they would rather steal, rob rather than work. It is a load of manure, absolute nonsense. The poor in town can hardly survive. They exhaust their credit; exhaust their friends, relatives and everyone. The roads are crowded with men and women ravenous for work, murderous for work. People move like ants in search of work, of food. But alas, it is like chasing a mirage.'

'And naturally the frustration and anger begin to foment. The line between hunger, anger and law-breaking is a very thin one. The choice is simply between survival and breaking the law. Crime in these circumstances makes a hell lot of sense. In a dog-eat-dog society where competition for survival is the order of the day, individuals must fend for themselves in order to live. The philosophy becomes that of cannibals: eat or be eaten. So the poor are trapped in a vicious cycle. They have nowhere to escape from it all. No one is making a significant effort to help. No one cares for the *povo,* the poor and hungry. To the rich and powerful they are only grains of sand. Who cares for grains of sand. Who loses sleep over grains of sand.'

This other young fellow with big protruding eyes decides to tell it like it is 'Doctor, you may think I am nuts but I believe strongly in abortion, and even baby dumping. All the pious mouthings of anti-abortion...anti-baby dumping advocates fall strangely silent in the face of those thousands of unwanted, unloved, unfed, unclothed and abused children. They all become deaf, dumb and blind. No one has the heart, the care and thought for them.'

'Ineffective but self-interested propaganda campaigns for the poor children hardly compare to the panic and terror that grip the poor, utterly resourceless. I grieve for the thousands who have died and will continue to die trapped in this nightmare. It haunts me. It is frightening. It is better to be dead than alive. The poet B.M. Themba is right when he says

Blessed are the dead For they will:
        Never be suspected,
        Never be chased,
        Never be unmanageable
        Never be transformed into
firewood
        Never be killed

For they are now:
        Protected from adversaries
        Saved from opponents,
        Secured from the persecution of this
world.
        Blessed are those who are dead.'

An admirer of Mother Teresa, the utterly selfless nun of world repute, cuts in with her saying: *'The biggest disease today is not leprosy or tuberculosis or aids, but rather the feeling of being unwanted, uncared for and deserted by everybody. The greatest evil is the lack of love and charity, the terrible indifference towards one's neighbour who lives at the roadside assaulted by exploitation, corruption, poverty and disease.'* With that the fellow frowns in sympathy and shuts up.

A former combatant in the war of liberation lashes out at the leaders in the country and in Africa. He, and

'the millions of Africa, are tired of pomposity, incompetence, totalitarianism and cupidity of the leaders whom they are condemned to live under. I note that politics at its best is a noble quest for a good order and justice but at its worst, a selfish grab for power, glory and riches. The latter is sadly what Africa has become. Most parties in Africa have taken their people for granted, and for a ride, usually on a one-party bandwagon. African politics is a farce. You see someone running, at election time, upside down with ballot boxes that have been tempered with. They intimidate, kill and trick to win elections.'

The leaders forget that they come from the people, belong to the people and should be destined for the people. No human being owns another human being. We are all on loan to each other, just as this beautiful continent, like earth, is on loan to us all.' He spreads his hands preacher style, staring into space

'But alas the behaviour of our leaders is counter to these noble tenets as well as universal truths. Only a generation ago, independence sowed hope across this continent. Alas, though independent we are not free. Africa is living through such difficult times that its very survival is in question. Africa is in danger of real death. It is in its death throes.'

'Independence, from colonial powers, has brought no liberty for millions of Africans. The rallying cry *one man one vote* has suffered a pathetic ironic twist. Many Africans have now one vote, but often it can be cast for only one man. Nationhood in Africa will too often continue to be a sad parody of itself. It is a conspiracy of human failure and nature: drought, even of leadership, earthquakes, floods, pests, disease and sheer mismanagement.' He folds his hands across his chest

'It is ironic that the departure of the white administration has led to disaster. Tribalism, nepotism, greed, unworthy leaders and half-baked ideologies have taken over and ruined the economy...ruined everything. And in the turmoil hundreds of thousands of people have been shot, stabbed, strangled, drowned, fed to crocodiles and hyenas, killed in stage-managed road accidents, tortured, maimed and burnt to death.'

'Alas no one raises a finger, a voice to help these victims of the horrific atrocities. The armies and secret police have been perverted by putting them in the hands of killers and cold-blooded murderers. Grovelling ambitious persons pander to the cruelties of the ruling elite. The ruling elite's wish becomes their command. Fear motivation, intimidation, bullying become standard practice. Hence , the countries become extermination, murder factories run on a ruthless campaign of intimidation and terror of innocents that makes *Murder Incorporated* appear like a Sunday school organisation. Africa is yet again slipping into the dark patches of its chequered history.' He unfolds his hands and looks at Dumba, with eyes full of bitterness

'Small wonder, Winston Churchill, with unusual foresight, opposed relinguishing power to Third World leaders: *Power will go into the hands of rascals, rogues and freebooters. Not a bottle of water or a loaf of bread will escape taxation. Only the air will be free, and the blood of these hungry millions will be on the head of the giver of independence. These are men of straw whom no trace will be found after a few years. They will fight among themselves, and the country will be lost in political squabbles...in turmoil.* At the time most people dismissed Churchill's dire prophecies as the rantings of an imperialist crackpot. Today there are many of us who totally agree that he was dead right.'

The ex-combatant continues without interruption from Dumba

'All too often, comrade, fledgling African democracies have become total hostage to leaders intent solely on gaining and holding on to power at all costs. Africa has its miniature Stalins, men who have unleashed reigns of terror the like of which independent Africa has seldom seen. They wield absolute power, and always fearful for their lives since their hands are full of blood, they become monsters of cruelty.'

'They regard themselves as rare and endangered species...the last borns of the world. Hence, they are constantly guarded by hordes of hand-picked soldiers armed to the teeth with super guns, ground to ground...surface to surface, surface to air and scud missiles. What a new degeneration!' His mood becomes prophetic

The triumph of independence from colonialism is a Pyrrhic victory for the African. All African states can become failing states overnight -infested with fragile economies, corruption, inefficiency, genocidal horrors. Wars of attrition, ethnic cleansing take over where hunger, and disease, have stopped. Cry the forsaken continent! Africa is in real danger of getting off the map. Where there seems to be some stability of state , it is the stability of the grave yard. But the miniature Stalins continue to hold sway oblivious of the havoc they wreak on the beleaguered continent.'

'Strangely these miniature Stalins speak up eloquently and persistently on behalf of freedom for the Africans in Southern Africa and the rest of the world. But this same man has turned his own country into a great terror. Meanwhile there is a deafening silence on the part of independent Africa to the terror in these states.' The young fellow spits with contempt

'Only once or twice has Africa broken the silence, the passive acquiescence to the atrocities, the crimes without a name. One, Mwalimu Julius Kambarage Nyerere selflessly, and gallantly booted out Idi Amin. I am no enthusiast for biological engineering; but I wish they could 'clone' Julius Kambarage Nyerere.'

Two, a leader at the Organisation Of African Unity meeting chastised Africa's silence when it comes to tyranny in Third World countries. He bravely lambasted them: *Tyranny is colour blind and should be no less reprehensible when it is perpetrated by one of our own kind. Death is death, and pain is pain regardless of the colour of the victim or the perpetrator. Africa's silence in the face of gross abuses of basic human rights undermines Africa's moral authority to condemn the excesses of others like the Pretoria apartheid regime. My brothers and sisters Africa has a sorry record in moral suasion and human rights. 1 must be honest with you. We must clean our own stinking house first.!* 'He concludes in exasperation

'Alas, do they hear? Do they listen? But learn they don't. It is a dialogue of the deaf. And, barring what is called an unforeseen circumstance, the self-anointed messiahs alias Stalins of Africa will be around for a long time. And their voices will continue to reverberate across Africa and beyond.'

'All the while, the poor African people will remain condemned to a twilight existence under totalitarian rule. For most Africans there is nowhere to go as political oppression takes its own savage toll. It is moral degeneracy, for what kind of leaders would oppress their people while making propaganda all round the world. If there is any specimen lower than a fornicating preacher, it must be a shady African leader.'

Yet another young fellow joins in with a comment meant for the whole world that seems to have lost its innocence and sense of justice

'Has there ever been an age that, considering its lights, has done worse things than this one, with its class hatreds, race hatreds, colour prejudices, world wars, civil wars, ethnic clashes bordering on genocide, and concentration camps? Has there been another age that, knowing so clearly the right things to do, merchantising humanity's finest feelings, has so consistently done the wrong ones? Is it because we are in a workshop of fate?'

Another ex-combatant rushes in with an astute but biting economic rejoinder. He points out that, potentially Africa, south of the Sahara, is a rich continent, endowed with natural resources such as land, minerals, fauna, flora and people. But most of the countries' coffers are empty, the currencies almost worthless. The lethal cocktail of tribalism, nepotism, corruption, mismanagement, religious strife has played havoc with Third World economies. He pauses for breath before continuing with the lecture

'We have politicians, leaders...adults farting around with the countries' economies to their destruction. They are termites, termites of the economy; devastating pests of national development. They make and leave us all orphans. '

'Doctor, Ours is a weary land dominated by plundering local cohorts without conscience...real bastards. People in great haste, hurrying to amass wealth, with whores, mistresses accommodated in apartments fitted out as sumptuous love-nests paid for from looted public funds. Meanwhile prices of commodities have been artificially rocketed and shortages are rampant. Our people are starving and they rely on international handouts albeit donor fatigue. Africa's starving children are saved by charitable people in developed countries whilst Africa's vampire elites watch, with overflowing larders at home and balances in Europe and America.'

'Meanwhile African women's breasts have shrunk to flaps, their bellies are a mass of wrinkles and folds...the children are skinny and pot-bellied pumpkins. Hunger has made them vicious and cruel, even to one another. They steal and rob food from the mouths of the old, the weak and the sick. It is heart-rending. It makes even hard-boiled field commanders fight welling tears in their eyes.'

'What should one say to the screaming children, as they are carried in their mothers' arms from the burning homes for shelter-seekers euphemistically called *squatter camps?* What should one say to the homeless, hapless and hungry children? Can we comfort them with promises of a better tomorrow? Who can feed on promises of tomorrow? Who can shelter under tomorrow?'

'If you have grown up as I did, this wouldn't surprise you. As our elders say, he who has drunk from a calabash can gauge its size. I have personal, direct experience of the dreadful life. Bedroom, living room, dining room, kitchen, playroom, nursery are *all* one room. Seven children in one room. Sex and laughter, hunger and joy, snot, tears - and boiling water - in one room!'

'Were it the stuff of Greek tragedy, the fates would be wheeled in as justification. When bad luck descends repeatedly, destructively, it begins to take on the prestige of a force above nature: a curse. But this is misery, fate and tragedy brought on other human beings by fellow mortals. You don't have to consult the medicine person, the spirit medium, the *sangoma,* the *sanyanga.* The witch, the cause is there...the African politician.'

Dumba listens carefully without interrupting the young men's flow of ideas. The young man clears his voice angrily and continues

'After a decade of falling per capita incomes, Africans are almost as poor today overall as they were thirty years ago. I've travelled all over Africa, you know. So I know what I'm talking about. Africa's track record has been a textbook example of imperious and impoverishing mismanagement in the developing world. The extent of mismanagement, waste and spending, the indifference to health, education, transport has left the continent a wasteland.'

'Birth, for many babies in Africa, is a sentence of death. Hunger progresses into starvation. A child was once asked what it would like to be. *Alive,* was the answer. These personal and political failures plague the continent.' He pauses for effect and continues

'And there is no reason to expect good news from Africa for a long time. For across this vast continent one zone of disaster elbows upon another. A sore-hit country has emerged from thirty years of anti-colonial struggle, but the next-door country continues to be plunged in conflict with itself; another riven apart by brigands and war lords; yet another wonders what comes next; while another land of lost horizons wagers hope against hope that its new won peace may hold. And millions stare into starvation. Africa, the beautiful continent is now entering the very heart of darkness.'

'Many reasons for this misery are found in human frailty and few derive from the unfavourable harsh international terms of trade. Such essential services as transport, health, education, communications are often in disarray. It's not uncommon to find trees growing in the middle of the tarmac road...potholes that can bury a whole bus right in the middle of the city. No wonder the discontent level has reached more than ninety five percent. The dependence on expatriate expertise in vital services is almost total.' He stops to sneeze and blow his nose. As he rubs the stuff on to his thigh he proceeds with his lecture

'All the while, because of dictatorship, of intolerance to dissenting opinion, of the ruined economies, Africa's brain drain accelerates at an alarming rate, hindering, if not crippling development. The flight of skilled people from Africa robs it of its best qualified personnel and intellectual resources. They flee and flock to prosperous lands thereby escaping persecution, ethnic tensions, intimidation, political insecurity, administrative ineptitude and abject poverty.'

'So the countries of Africa continue to be infested with expatriates, many of them with dubious qualifications, spanning all sectors of the economy. Those locals who remain in the system are usually the chaff, the dregs that rise to the top...producing the *chibuku* rough beer *effect.* '

This ex-combatant is a real talker. He pauses to refer to some notes. His dry tongue conies out searching for moisture around his lips. It finds none.

'Africa's decay also extends to projects and equipment built and financed by not so well meaning foreign nations. In many countries technological white elephants have proliferated. No group has lavished more on grandiose schemes, and has less to show for it, than Africa's leaders and their bureaucracies. Meanwhile thousands in slums of cities lack running water, adequate sewage systems, transport, medical care and educational facilities. All these are swept under the carpet in lies, in excuses, in censored news, in suppression of popular opinion.' He chides

'When a government deceives and defrauds its own people, it commits a crime of the highest degree. As if this deception is not enough, summary execution, torture, arbitrary arrests, exile or prolonged detention without trial are the common experience of academics in African countries. This culture of violence, this total disregard of people's basic human needs and rights is a tragic way of life for millions whose needs will last far longer than the next appeal for help.'

'It is hunger that cries out beyond appeal. It is hunger for food, for peace, for freedom, for basic human rights, for shelter, for the basics of life. But nobody cares for they are only grains of sand to be trampled upon without care. It is a weary land dominated by plundering cohorts. They are deaf and dumb and blind to the cries for justice, fairness, equality, the development of truth, of objectivity that allows us to be self-critical. The call for people whose only masters are two: the truth, their own consciences, to hold public office is scorned. The litany of cheating and mismanagement, of grudges, hatred and vendettas, of misrule, of corruption stink up to heaven. It is treason, genocide, a crime without a name. It shames and embarrasses.'

'Such a government forfeits the reason and purpose for its own existence and continuance in office. Its leaders lose irretrievably the right and privilege to command. There must be an orderly, peaceful transfer of power in the best interests of the governed.'

'But alas this does not normally happen because the regimes are not only ruthless and corrupt but extravagant, careless and incompetent. They have killed. Their hands are dripping with blood. They fear the same fate will befall them. They cling to power at all costs to avoid the inevitable uncovering and exposure.'

'So it's not out of charity but out of self-interest, self preservation and survival that they hang on to power. It is not the wise way but the African political way. Another reason is that power corrupts and absolute power is absolutely delicious. And the snout of the beast really conies out to protect that sweet power, that is more delicious than the rich African honey.'

'So you find corruption is pandemic in government, right up to the top, in parastatals and quasi-private enterprises. Corruption by individuals, government and business is a pandemic mental illness. Milk cows, in the form of parastatals, quasi-private enterprises are set up by the ruling elites to facilitate the theft and channeling of funds into banks overseas.'

'The leaders of government and captains of commerce and industry form the vampire elites who make huge profits by manipulating regulations, selling import licences and extorting unauthorised fees, soliciting and accepting bribes, cuts and kickbacks. They are more exploitative than the colonial masters of the past, consuming more and contributing less if not very little. Because of them Africa buys dear and sells cheap. They leave us drained of resources. They leave us dry grains of sand...a grey mass, a nothing.' He blows his nose furiously before going on

'Africa is bankrupt, given over to self-serving politicians and crazy leaders and de facto one-party presidents-for-life...full of grandiose slogans and paranoid whining; holding out their tin cups to all the 'affluent' nations, yet knowing full well the pockets that most of the 'aid' disappears into. All society becomes infested with predatory corruption.'

'Africa is also very bankrupt of leaders (take me to your leader!). The most destructive people rise to power to control all affairs of state. Politicians rise to ruin entire nations. These parasitical-elite humanoids inflict purposeful harm on conscious beings, their economies, their lives and their societies. The worst economic and social harms are inflicted on society. The parasitical elites manipulate nearly all politics, bureaucracies, the legal profession, the academe, the news media, religion, entertainment and the state apparatus. What those manipulators represent as the best is really the worst...the most destructive.'

'For Africa has the misfortune to have irremovable presidents who take elaborate measures to defend themselves against popular anger with electric fences, as if they are rare royal game, close circuit television, observation and security towers, vicious dogs, alarm systems, guards. Only cowards need that kind of protection.'

'And the presidents never divulge their intentions, as they travel from their state house prisons by helicopter. There are lots of horrors that cry out for abolition or alleviation, devils that need exorcism.'

'And as if Africa has not enough troubles already, now it has the new horror of AIDS. And then to look at all this corruption, unemployment, crime (of the rich and powerful) and prostitution is to despair for the future of Africa. Africa seems to have no defence against crazy thimble-rigging politicians acting Jehovah by day light. Until it has, there is very little hope for it. Africa is pretty sick so it urgently needs political pills, economic surgery, and moral remedies.'He clutches his knee.

The countries are incapable of ensuring an honest civil service or police force. Incapable of pulling themselves up by their own bootstraps; if they have any bootstraps, after a generation of independence. Corruption from top to bottom is as serious a haemorrhage everywhere in Africa now as slavery was up to a century ago; and very much more difficult to abolish. There is no civic conscience as public money is faceless and nameless. Africa takes bribes with enthusiasm. Dash or bribe is now the custom of Africa with most people, workers, too poor to be honest.

He pauses for air and winds his long, barbed, caustic lecture on a hopeful note

'But Africa has to emerge from pain and ruin. What is the route of escape from present disasters? The route must pass through genuine democratic involvement in self-administration by the people, that is in mass participation not mass manipulation. The African state must be rescued from its neo-colonial misery and rigid centralism, of ruling by subterfuge, by brute force. We must be rescued, by none but ourselves, from a revolution that has gone rabid, that has turned on itself, that has turned on its head.'

'There is salvation in Africa herself for once she has shined! During the European Middle Ages Africa showed itself perfectly capable of, and better at organising large and complex socio-economic and political structures, based on technologies, large enough and stable enough to be called empires, and congenial and benign enough to deserve the names of sophistication and civilisation, with a good measure of literacy.'

Dumba listens intently to yet another devastating critique of failure, which apportions blame all round, but reserves its harshest criticism for the senior echelons of African government. The venom is direct and stunning. The speaker stings. It is direct inoculation.

'Doctor, unless you have experienced tyranny, you cannot fully appreciate how wonderful freedom is. You cannot appreciate light without darkness. The rulers are no benevolent despots. They rule by rage, by subterfuge. They think with the spinal cord...with their sex organs. They are primitive savages. They never know when to depart from power. They never heed the wise words from the statesman Mwalimu Nyerere: *When you see your neighbour being shaved, you should wet your beard and head...Otherwise you get a very rough painful shave.* Nor do they heed the ageless African advice to one taking public office: let *no one say, and say it to your shame, that all was well and beauty here until you came.'*

This young fellow really knows how to castigate crimes of the powerful that go unchecked and unpunished. He goes on to assert that

'the criminal activities of the poor and powerless are a tiny drop in the ocean compared with the huge sums criminally and illegally pocketed by the powerful. So the real criminals in this society are *not* the people who populate the prisons across the state, but those people who steal the wealth of the state from the people. Those are the people who should be incarcerated for keeps here in jail, not you and I. Those are the people who should be kept in prison till the donkey and baboon have grown horns...till snakes walk on four legs...till the snake has buttocks, buttocks as big as mine.' He illustrates the size by holding his big behind in both hands.

A tall lanky fellow with rickety legs joins in the discussion rather abruptly and unceremoniously. The gap left when his legs are tightly close together allows soccer balls to pass through freely and in quick succession. He wouldn't make a good goal keeper. But his views are straight. He thinks that the leaders deserve a severe chastisement. They have sinned badly. Hence a good chastisement is like a good sermon; it must not only comfort the afflicted, it must also afflict the comfortable.

'The basic source of the problem is that there are two sets of laws in this country. The occasional prosecution of ruling class crime provides the fiction, the myth, that the law operates for the benefit of society as a whole, and that the extent of ruling class crime is small. In any case the powerful quickly rescue each other from going to prison.'

'Help, by the ruling elite, is more often given to friends, relatives, attractive persons, and people perceived as being similar to the helpers. So the use of selective pardons and selective justice is quite common. Commissions of inquiry are often used as a charade and a clever cover up.'

'Defining the poor and powerless who break the powerful's laws as *animals, misfits, enemies of the state,* provides a justification for incarcerating them in prisons. This keeps them hidden from view, from the public eye.'

'In this way the most embarrassing extremes produced by the heinous system are neatly swept under the carpet. By keeping its victims so thoroughly hidden and rendering them inhuman, the evil system is sustained.' The lanky fellow's eyes and tone change menacingly. He stabs the air with his index finger.

'But let me warn them. They are making a big mistake. The higher the platform the harder the fall! The spider will get entangled in its own web. It will get ensnared in its own trap. The African Nemesis, the goddess of retribution and vengeance, the righteous wrath, the comeuppance will descend on them without mercy. They will score an own goal of World Cup standards that will stand to shame them forever.'

'Crimes do not die. Those committing them are answerable in terms of natural law of justice. For even in our silence, even when there are no fora for our voices the ruling elite cannot censor our thoughts. They cannot imprison our hunger for freedom. They cannot exile our sense of justice, or murder the very essence that carries our bleeding protests through walls and prisons.'

'So in the end, it is time itself that is against them and time is a very powerful enemy. Not even the ruling elite can sensor, imprison, exile or murder time. Tune is the midwife of history. They could and have changed the chapters; changed the book but the story remains the same.' The fellow's eyes smart with wrath

'Their love of power, name, status, wealth has risen to dangerous levels. And these are the circumstances that invite deception, and in turn disaster. Gangs of organised thieves take the state hostage. This is the madness that eventually brings destruction to Africa. What they forget is that although humans may respect these things, the *truth* does not. What they lose sight of, in the smugness of success, in the sweetness of power is that the truth is no respecter of hierarchy or fame. It can come out of the mouths of mere underlings, like you the valiant Dumba, our doctor.' He issues his threats, again with the aid of his fingers, AK rifle style

The ruling elite will find out that the trodden, despised grains of sand will one day fill their dirty mouths, grate their bloody teeth, blunt their crimson fangs, travel down their clogged throats...their stinking gullets and choke them. The venom of the people will finish them off. Remember the white colonial regimes we beat? We made them bite the dust. What makes these African bastards think we can't do the same, if not worse, to them hey?' The warning persists undisguised

'You must give the tortoise time to put out its head before you can catch hold of it. Unpopular ideas have a way of coming into their own in the long run. They forget that life being what it is, we are all in the soup together. And events would arrange themselves in such a way as to make everyday more inevitable. Events will spell doom for them. For at the bottom of every bully and tyrant lurks a coward.'

Yet another fellow briefly comments on the tyranny, hypocrisy, cruelty, cupidity and cunning of the African leaders. He feels the destiny of nations is often swayed by the faulty blood pressure of dictators. Dictators who are heavily drunk for years on end with power, that fiercest of intoxicants. Dictators who approach political matters with the breeziest of bed-side manners, as if the entire world is their patient. They diagnose, prescribe, attempt to conquer. They are used to having their own way, urged on by flatterers, sycophants, and cheer leaders but haunted by the fact that they have very little time left. So they take steps which prove to be their greatest blunders. He illustrates his point

'Take this leader's policy in regard to the land question. It might justly be considered a triumph of stupidity. He considers that the goose that lays golden eggs ought never to be allowed to cackle. His view is that although these people have enriched his treasury, they have enriched themselves much more. He forgets that he, and his hench-persons, have created the mess the country is in.'

'Their government is not only repressive but greedy, dishonest, corrupt, inefficient, wasteful and ridiculous. Bribery and nepotism are rampant...the tax-payer's money is wasted...there is interference with the courts. Petitions are treated with contempt. They glorify petty tyrannies, extort money and women. They hold the crude belief that the welfare of the country can be permanently based on fear felt by the majority for a powerful ruling elite.'

'The inability to see any point of view but their own has become a national curse. It makes them overbearing, intolerant and rude. They have lost most of any faculty for self-criticism. They display the arrogance of a person who has been poisoned by power. Their arrogance leads to megalomania.' He ends on a prophetic note

'But one thing is certain. These temporary masters of people will become servants of destiny. They do not know that they undertake their extraordinary tasks as a matter of course. For time, destiny, the future belong to the people, us. We are the natural winners.'

The last words come from a comical character. He approaches Dumba rather cautiously feeling like a person trying to back away from a poised cobra without causing it to strike. He is cynical par excellence. He remarks that

'a world without tyrants would be as boring as a zoo without hyenas. Bullying is a classic example of tyranny of the weak. Tyrants have a great knowledge of people. Though criminally insane they are not fools. They know just how to manipulate people. You can't be a tyrant and an imbecile at the same time. Tyrants are like scientists: they are always experimenting, to see how far they can go. They always advance until the very end, until the moment everything falls apart.'

'So three quarters of history is the history of tyranny, of slavery, of human misery. Unfortunately this is our situation, our plight but, fortunately, not our fate.' He admonishes

'The other cause of the present African condition is that of blind imitation. Imitation is the sincerest form of flattery. When Africans were second and third rate citizens in their own countries they instinctively imitated the white colonial masters in many things. Unfortunately they tended to imitate them in all the wrong things instead of the right things. So an educated, or half- or quarter-educated African desires to give orders to inferiors and shuns working with own hands. S/he wishes to acquire the white person's authority without the white person's efficiency, sense of civic integrity and honesty.'

'Even the most senior whites lived modestly and frugally. But when an African makes it to the top of the heap s/he feels no inclination even to pretend simplicity and modesty. S/he lives infantile fantasies, builds himself palaces of sybaritic grandeur, surpassing Disneyland and Coney Island put together. S/he becomes sophisticated before s/he is civilised.'

'But next door to him lives the former white master in a simple plain house, accessible to all. Small wonder we are in a mess, we are bankrupt? Independence, without freedom for us, has meant we are now more dependent than ever on the former colonial nations.'

'But Doctor mark my words. Though we are nothing but grains of sand to them we are the eventual natural winners. Truth, justice, hope and fairness are an inseparable part of us.'

He ends with a didactic message to the leaders. This fellow surprises Dumba by quoting very intelligently and appropriately Kishore Mahbubani's Ten Commandments for Development in the Third World:

1.Thou shall blame only thineself for thine failures in development.
Blaming imperialism, colonialism and neo-colonialism is a convenient
excuse to avoid self-examination

2.Thou shall acknowledge that corruption is the single most important cause for failures in development. Developed countries are not free from corruption. With their affluence, they can afford to indulge in savings-and-loans scandals. REMEMBER developing countries cannot

3.Thou shall not subsidise any products. Nor punish the farmer to favour the unproductive or the city-dweller. If there are food riots, resign from office. Thou has lost thine mandate to rule because the population does not believe that only they should make sacrifices when their leaders make none

4.Thou shall abandon state control for free markets. Have faith in thine own people. When their fetters are removed, they shall go forth and produce. An alive and productive population naturally lead to development

5.Thou shall borrow no more. Get foreign investment that pays for itself. Build only the infrastructure that is needed. Create no white elephants nor monuments nor roads that end in deserts. Accept the results of independent *feasibility studies. Accept no aid that is only intended to subsidise ailing industries in developed countries. Disband all 'milk* cows', *enterprises meant to divert funds to personal accounts in Europe and America*

6.Thou shall not reinvent the wheel. Millions of people on this planet have gone through the path of development. Take the well travelled roads. Be not prisoners of dead irrelevant ideologies

7.Thou shall scrub the ideas of a 19th century German Jew philosopher called Karl Marx out of thine mind and systems and replace them with the ideas of pragmatism. The Germans, the Jews have made their choice. We should follow suit

8.Thou shall be humble when developing. Humility is no sin. It is an essential ingredient for learning Do not expend your energies lecturing the developed world on their sins of commission and omission. They politely listened in the 1960's and 1970's. They no longer will in the present and future

9.Thou shall abandon all North- South forums. Such fora only encourage hypocritical speeches and token gestures. Remember that countries which have received the greatest amount of aid per capita have failed most spectacularly in development. Throw out of the window all theories of superfluous development

10.Thou shall not abandon HOPE. People are the same all over the world. What the west achieved yesterday, the developing world will achieve tomorrow. It can be DONE!

Dumba is left in no doubt that the whole system needs overwhelming overhaul. There is need for a fresh start to escape the self-inflicted disasters in Third World states. The justice area is one example that needs very urgent attention. The upsurge in prison populations is a symptom of a decaying, collapsing society.

The blame also lies squarely on the tardiness of the country's judicial system. Unethical and improper practices by a large number of state judicial and police officers contribute to prison congestion and the attendant problems. Bribery and corruption are common at the magistrate level. Most magistrates and some judges are fond of sending people to jail without an option of a fine. They are most unwilling to apply suspended sentences which are accepted all over the civilised world as some of the most effective ways of decongesting prisons.

Imprisonment should be restricted to offenders from whom the public needs safe-guarding. Probation, parole, suspended sentences, restitution orders and work releases to cover those involved in non-violent crimes like fraud, embezzlement and cheating should suffice instead of incarceration. This will go a long way in emptying these cages of human tragedy.

Though we know that common sense is not that common, leaders should show some form of morality and conscience to appreciate the plight of common suffering people. People who call themselves, and feel that they are, grains of sand. The grains of sand must become the basis, the foundation, the building block, the seed bed of change and development.

Granted that Africa was carved up with boundaries made without consulting it as to its desires in the matter. There are now about forty countries south of the Sahara. Not one of them can be regarded as inherently stable. Not a single one is homogeneous within its own boundaries. Not one is a natural ethnic entity. Not one is within normal boundaries. So Africa is a thing made, a white person's artefact. It is not an organic thing. The states are the wrong shape, the wrong size and too small and fragmented to be economically viable.

The African demagogues who inherit these pieces of land seem happy with the situation. It gives them the area of operations and myopic ambitions that they jealously guard like vicious dogs with juicy bones. There is no talk of some kind of rational rearrangement of boundaries, peoples and frontiers. So from the look of things Africa is bogged down with the illogical for the foreseeable future.

One hopes that African leaders see and implement the examples, set by Europe, Americas, South East Asia, and the Pacific Rim, of breaking down economic barriers in favour of trading blocks. Likewise African nations must quickly combine into natural regional economic communities before their economies reach a point of no return.

Twelve

RISE AND WALK

More often than not prison life becomes so dreary, heavy going, and mental energy sapping. Inmates become weary of imprisonment. Sleep is in short supply. By now nerves are rattled; friends snap at one another. Tempers flare and the social atmosphere becomes steamy and charged with emotion. Appetites fall but in some cases they grow abnormally high. There is lack of concentration at work and study. Morale falls to its lowest ebb. One can almost hear the silent weeping of the heart: *my unhappiness is a bottomless cup...deliver me from my dismal swamp of despair.*

When situations reach such low levels the prison authorities call in the Padre to counsel privately and also publicly. This time the Padre is on sick leave so he is not available. They decide Dumba should help out because of his training and professional background.

Dumba has also had enough of the bickering and squalor, the petty thieving and betrayals that spoil the lives of people locked up together like rats in a wired cage. So he also thinks it a pretty good idea to put an end to the anxiety of people rotting in their cages. He has to extinguish a small, but extremely dangerous, glow of hatred before it grows into a flame, a conflagration.

Dumba holds private counselling sessions with the most serious cases. He, however, decides to also utilise the group counselling approach in a form of a *pep* talk. He feels that the youngsters need motivation, reassurance and *pep* talk in this emotional area of their lives. So he goes.

'Young men, life is not just bread and butter issues. Life is an up-hill struggle. Life is not always fair. Remember that it is life that gives us our first taste of suffering and tragedy. We must survive the most brutal conditions life, through people, can dish out. There is nothing at all strange and absurd about the human condition. What is very important is that we matter. We are the newest, the youngest, and the brightest thing around.'

'Softies will sink and drown in the hazardous depths of life's stormy currents. Those who are not strong enough, mentally and physically, will be swept under. A hero is known only on the battle field. So the heroism of life can be discovered in the battle of life. You must take courage for no amount of weeping, moaning, mourning and self-deprecating will make you get out of jail. Problems don't have wings to bear them away.'

'In fact research, and the school of life, have shown that the trials of life are far less important than how one deals with them. As the well worn saying goes *when the going gets tough, the tough get going.* People who survive and succeed in life learn to fight and overcome crises. They find themselves in tough, punishing circumstances and bravely overcome them.'

They are struck down by illness and catastrophe. They are assailed by grief and failure. They are treated unfairly or they are betrayed. They are severely handicapped and may be buried alive in their apparently useless bodies. Yet from the prison of their useless bodies soars an invincible spirit that is to touch the hearts of, and benefit, millions. Yet they not only survive. They confront their stresses and sorrows in ways that deepen and enrich their lives. They go on with courage, distinction and grace. You may ask what is the secret of their survival? There are no secrets in life and living. It is prudence, sheer guts and commonsense. The techniques are simple yet so effective. Here are the techniques'

'*One,* make happiness a habit. You must enjoy life even when troubles and problems spring up like thistles in a patch of weeds. Take each day as it comes, full of sorrow, joy, disappointment and surprise. When you cannot have the big victory, accept small ones. And you should learn to know where to look for a flash of excitement, the moment of insight and beauty. Even concentration camp survivors tell of small pleasures that kept them sane - a glowing sunset, the moonlight, the sound of a bird, of an insect, of wind.'

The tenacious hold on life to survive; a strength as stubborn as the upsurge of spring made even holocaust victims pull through some of the harshest conditions of life. For you to succeed in life you should have a talent for life, a fury and a desire to use all of it.'

To suffer is to succeed. Yes it is true that to slip is not to fall, to stumble is not to fall down but to go forward. So you should treasure the time that is. You should find each day's joys and miracles of life, however small. My teacher of philosophy was fond of telling us that suffering is just about the easiest of human activities. Being happy is just about the hardest. You know it is true. No one is born happy. Everyone makes his or her own happiness by having the will to live and be happy.'

The German statesman Count Bismark once remarked that we should not only strike while the iron is hot but we should make the iron hot by striking. Yes, my dear young fellows, we must strike out happiness right now by smiling. Wear a smile. One size fits all. Yes let us laugh right away. I am eternally happy that you are all smiling and laughing. This is the way to do it. Laughter, like happiness, is really a very personal experience. It has to start with the individual, though it can become a group experience. But first it has to work for you... then it can work in a crowd. Each one of us can be a source of happiness or sorrow, which ever we decide to choose. Laughter is not only the best medicine but the panacea to stress and unhappiness.'

'*Two,* accept change. Problems and change will come whether we want them or not. As we approach each unthinkable catastrophe or disaster, it strangely becomes thinkable. For problems are solutions in disguise. Time is the best problem solver. For with time what appeared insurmountable becomes surmountable. Life is all but change. So accept change, not with resignation but with a fierce longing to learn from it.'

'When our lives explode, like the universe, they come together in new patterns. What looks like disaster may turn out to be the best thing that ever happens to us. For a start, here we are learning together and from each other. We become wiser, richer in our lives and experiences. Please note that every experience is a good one provided we survive it and learn from it. Change is nine times out of ten better for us, good for our personal development.'

'*Three,* never, never give up. Never, never despair. Do not give up. You may be in the eye of the storm or in the midst of the tempest. Despite being afraid or blocked by obstacles, to survive you must quietly do what has to be done. Do not be intimidated. Never say die. Be calm and act positively no matter how overwhelming the odds against you. Do not give up the good fight. Be a resolute fighter, a survivor and winner - all in one. Keep on trying, and trying and trying...until you succeed.'

The power to work hard may not be talent, but it is the best possible substitute for it. Don't waste time and effort telling the world what you are going to do - just do it. When you have thoroughly made up your mind about anything you should be like an elemental force, like a stream of water which progresses through, round or over any obstacles which it cannot sweep before it. Seize at opportunities that come your way. Opportunity seldom knocks at any one's door with a sledge hammer, and a golden one at that. Rarely, it is as if fate itself would have intervened. So make the best out of every opportunity that arises.'

'Also reach out to others. When your woes and troubles threaten to overcome you, think about how you can help someone else.'

'*Four*, live in the present. Stop living for a distant tomorrow and begin appreciating the glories of each day. Life lies in letting go, in giving up your grievances. You should avoid eating your heart out. Avoid worrying. It is the cancer of thinking. Worry is like a rocking chair. It keeps you going but it takes you nowhere.'

'*Five*, be your own best friend. Be kind to your own system. If we spend our precious energies being angry with the people who once disappointed us, we will not have any left over for what we need now. Lost energy, like lost time, is a terrible, unforgiven waste.'

'Not one of us can bring back yesterday. Only today is ours and it will not be ours for long. Once it is gone, it will never in all time be ours again. So time, energy, life like love are scarce and precious commodities. They must be saved, treasured and utilised fully. For they are indeed vital resources that must be conserved and made use of wisely.'

'*Six*, do not be afraid to dream. Be on top of life, bright and vibrant, full of dreams and promise. To survive and succeed in life your life jacket should be made of the imperishable things with which you surround yourself. It could be books, music, spiritual faith, a purpose, a dream.'

'Books, for instance, abound with inspiration. These are not just books, lumps of life-less paper, but minds alive on the leaves and pages. From each of them goes out its own voice...and just as the touch of a button on our set will fill the room with music, so by taking down one of these volumes and opening it, one can call into range the voice of a person far distant in time and space, and hear the person speak to us, mind to mind, heart to heart. Literature is the honey of a nation's soul, preserved for her children to taste forever, a little at a time.'

'*Seven*, you must have ambition, positive ambition. You have to walk and live with a dream. Remember that survivors are ambitious people whose dreams come true as success. Great people you see around, and read about, are fuelled by dreams, by ambition. So it is quite healthy to dream good and big. It is no more a sin to be ambitious, to be great and rich...it is a miracle. Your incarceration here affords you an opportune time to plan and think out your life, even to just dream. Remember, dreams come true. Yes, they do you know!

'*Eight*, learn to overcome fear and guilt. We must handle adversity with fortitude. Fear and guilt are both very real natural feelings. To tackle them you have to accept your own humanity...that human beings are often weak and afraid, that we have all done things of which we feel ashamed. You have made some mistakes, but who has not ? Show me one person who claims he has never made a mistake and I will show you a liar.'

True, people have memories and have to deal with the past, just as countries have to take into account their histories. There is no sin nor folly in dealing with the past. The folly arises when we try to live in it. To be human, and adult, is to remember ghastly times, cringe-making incidents, defeats, days in our lives when we should have played this card instead of that. We all have those awful re-runs of what we ought to have said when we lost the job, woman, friend, contract, freedom. We blew it. Or did we ? In my own life, it is the times when painful things happened, when I made a bad mistake, that led me to really reassess what I wanted , what I needed.'

'Bad things happen to us. It's true. It is what we make of the painful experience that is crucial. Bad, nasty experiences can give us the impetus to change our lives. They can lead us to figure out, possibly for the first time, who we really are and what we vitally need. All human beings look inwards and backwards. That is fine - as long as you learn to look outwards, positively and forward.'

'If you commit some terrible crime you should feel guilty, and mend your ways. The worst guilt is the self imposed guilt with which we sentence ourselves. Some people feel guilty about just being alive. Guilt, in itself, does nothing except to stop us thinking clearly and acting wisely. You committed no crime of magnitude. You acted a bit daft, were a bit wet, were too dependent, weak. If you are guilty so am I...so are lots of other people. You did what you could do then. You can do a lot better now.'

'You are going to learn to be brave but remember that brave people feel guilty and frightened too. The difference between the weak in character and the brave is that both feel fear, dismay, panic but the brave get in there and do it. So I invite you to say, *it hurt* (it did). Say *I have learnt something from it* (I think you have). Shout, *feeling guilty solves nothing* (it does not). Say loudly, *what is needed now is action!* (we are agreed on that completely).'

'It is a learning process and it is very scary but the rewards are tremendous. So please learn from your experience. Turn that negative into positive. Be brave and confident and live your life. No, you do not need to lean, like a broken pillar, on anybody. You are fine. You are all right. You are great, so get to

the starting line. Sprint for life. Today. Now!. Go into the orbit of
life. Grow and bloom where you are planted. Do not delay. Go into it
right away. Action person, now!'

'*Nine*, Forgive yourself, forget the guilt, banish the fear.
Tackle that fear by moving up to the starting line. Make new
friends and consolidate the old friendships. Be you, be honest, be
upright. The ability to progressively disclose your weaknesses, fears
and strengths to those you care about is the cement that holds love
and friendship together.'

'Above all, you have to be your own best friend to be really
happy. Hug yourself. You only live and lead one life. There is no need
to fuss about life since you do not come out of it alive anyway.'

'I must conclude by acknowledging that it is not easy to be a
fighter and a survivor, but it is always worth the effort. If we can live
our lives well in suffering, in hardships, in failure or
imprisonment...if we can use all our talents and determination, then
something of great worth will emerge and be added to the common
good.'

The wise people tell us that this longing to beat the odds, to
conquer our own weakness, to dream of a better world, has carried
humanity through its long chequered but exciting history. It is the
cry of the heroic in all of us. So it must guide and sustain us. I
believe we are the sum total of all our experiences - good and bad.
So whatever happens to us must not sink us. We must rise and walk.'

'Before I go I would like to leave you with these immortal
words, from Rudyard Kipling's poem If -

If you can keep your head when all about you
Are losing theirs and blaming it on you; If
you can trust yourself when all persons doubt you,
But make allowance for their
doubting too; If you can wait and not be
tired by waiting,
Or being lied about, don't
deal in lies, Or being hated don't
give way to hating,
And yet don't look too good, nor talk too wise:

If you can dream - and not make dreams your master;

If you can think - and not make thoughts
your aim, If you can meet with Triumph and
Disaster
        And treat those impostors just the
same; If you can bear to hear the truth
you've spoken
            Twisted by knaves to make a trap for fools,
            Or watch the things you gave your life to, broken,
                And stoop and build 'em up with worn-out tools:

If you can make one heap of all your winnings
        And risk it on one turn of pitch-and-toss, And lose,
and start again at your beginnings
        And never breathe a word about your loss; If you can
force your heart and nerve and sinew
        To serve your turn long after they are gone, And so hold
on when there is nothing in you
            Except the Will which says to them: 'Hold on !'

If you can talk with crowds and keep your virtue,
        Or walk with Kings - nor lose the common touch, If neither
foes nor loving friends can hurt you,
        If all persons count with you, but none too much; If you can
fill the unforgiving minute
        With sixty seconds' worth of distance run, Yours is the
Earth and everything that's in it,
            And- which is more - you'll be a Person, my child

Thirteen

CATHARSES

Every Sunday, the inmates have the whole day to themselves. They are left to their own devices. Facing and grappling with time, waiting, anxiety and emotions, is an uphill struggle. Time passes at a painful, punishing slow pace. It unloads tick by tick, droplet by droplet, tidbit by tidbit. It is like emptying a ten ton lorry of sand using a teaspoon or a fork for a shovel. In prison, like in captivity, minutes are hours, hours days, days weeks, weeks months and months years. Hey, time and emotions are locked in a life and death struggle.

Dumba passes the time by reliving his life in the tiniest detail. Besides the need to kill time inmates socialise and in the process reduce stress. The coping strategies include the usual stress reducers such as music: the lubricant of the troubled soul; dance: the relaxant of stretched muscles; gossip: the opium of the idle mind...games, sport, religious associations. Occasionally you have instances of drug taking, aggression and homosexuality. It is a micro-society with its own norms, values and ethos. Social life revolves on companionships through associations of various kinds. So is this Sunday.

In one corner of the prison ground is gathered a cosmopolitan group of youths performing and playing music on some old but effective string and wind instruments. The tunes move from jazz, funk, folk, carol, pop, blues, reggae, kasa kasa to country music. Surely you have Bongoman, Marley, Reeves, and Rogers equivalents here belting and wailing it out.

Next to them is a traditional dance troupe trotting out, stomping, galloping and tip-toeing one cultural dance after another. A few metres from them are two pairs of chess grand masters locked in battles of wits, moves, counter moves and tactical manoeuvres. Close to them is a group engaged in sheer idle talk spiced with stories of bravery, valour, love won and lost, cowardice and conquest. All in the mind perhaps but all the same very entertaining.

In the centre are two soccer teams putting all they have into the game. You have dribbling wizards, ball jugglers, sharp shooters and goal keepers who can make it to the *World Cup* finals. Here is real gem, real talent ready for the picking. The referee is a young fellow well known for his whistling talent. He backs up the spoken commands with superb imitation of referees' whistles.

There is 'radio' coverage of the game with the commentator, perched on a make-shift stand, giving a ball by ball run. In a fast high pitched voice he tells the listeners that United's goal keeper dives a shade too late as the ball trickles into the net to the thunderous applause of the goal-hungry supporters...

'City one, United zero. City one, United zero...The second half sees United fire the warning shots with some exciting exchanges which leave the City defence mesmerised and flat footed. Dear listeners, it is magic, pure magic. Now Tiki tries hard to pierce the City defence but finds the City goal minder in brilliant form. His effort is parried for a corner kick.'

'Again Tiki attacks again...Yes it's a g-o-a-1! Oh no. Tiki's attempt to emulate Diego Maradona's 'the hand of God' score with his hand in the 1986 World cup does not escape the hawk eyes of the referee, who disallows the goal. Dear listeners, this is a thriller. It's a gem. It is action packed.'

This time it is United's turn to be tested as United keeper is called upon to make a full stretch dive to save United from Chisa's rifled thunderous shot from thirty metres. The see-saw continues as United search for an equaliser but as yet in vain.' Dumba finds it comical, funny, creative and highly entertaining. What a world? What a People?

At the back is the small local congregation of a religious sect somewhere between a revival church and apostolic faith healers. They call themselves the *Church of Revelations*. They are about thirty in number. They gather every Sunday, for what they call the sabbath service. The service opens with a public confession of faults and personal sins. All members of the congregation present must pass through a 'gate' between two prophets. As each does so, he is supposed to mention aloud all his sins of the previous week. The prophets may add to the list if they 'see' faults the penitent fails to mention.

A common fault, confessed even by prophets, is loan sharking of cigarettes. Cigarettes are the currency of prison transaction. Steps are taken by the prophets to cleanse the sinner, which process consists of sprinkling of holy water, and a short prayer. The procedure exposes, and accepts, quarrels and other forms of malevolence in the church fraternity. It shows a public effort to improve the situation. It is fascinating to watch this gathering of worshipers.

The prophets speak in a lilting voice and utter groans, sighs and other sounds muffled down their throats. Possessed and overcome by the Holy Spirit they twitch and shake. They utter an incomprehensible jumble of names and phrases from the Bible, even from the Koran. Some of them seem to be even from Hindu. The Holy Spirit is believed to bestow on the prophets the gifts of speaking in tongues. At the service, a number of lay people enter into a kind of trance. The trance is induced by the rhythmic singing and the emotional preaching and praying of the assembly. They jabber in incomprehensible tongues. In this state both prophet and layperson can divine, prophesy, faith-heal and exorcise evil spirits and demons.

The sabbath service consists mainly of bible reading and preaching. Each preacher has a lector who reads from a chosen passage of the bible, a verse at a time. Every pertinent word is verbally underlined, and each verse is followed by comment from the preacher. The preaching is from time to time interrupted by the members breaking into rhythmic singing. They all sing, gyrate, trot and dance at a fast striding pace in tight circles. The way they twist, turn and jump would make even an experienced gymnast go dizzy. Some launch themselves into the air, and remain there, making one wonder when they are going to land.

A number of those present may fall into a trance, encouraged by prophets, and speak in strange tongues and prophesy. The service lasts for hours. It ends when all kneel down facing east praying aloud at the top of their lungs. They say their own impromptu prayers all at once imploring God to hear and answer their prayers. Silence means the answer is no!

After the service, water is consecrated for healing purposes. Healers of repute may lay their hands on the sick, who bring themselves forward, or are carried by friends or relatives. Those specially gifted pray for them and ask for God-speed recovery.

When it is *Pascal service,* which Dumba observes falls every two months, specially smuggled bread and fruit juice, representing wine, are taken towards the end of a similar service to the normal weekly services. It is a communion service preceded by baptisms in river *Jordan* symbolised by water in a bin. Those undergoing the ritual have their heads, held by the neck like a chicken going for slaughter, deftly dipped and immersed in water five times. It is quite a show of bravery to have one's head made to disappear in a bin full of water five times. Any way they survive it and they seem to enjoy it.

The communion service includes a foot washing ceremony by the pastor. This is followed by an address by the senior man present. He makes a little show of arranging and rearranging the containers of the communion. Then they all file past the communion table - a flat stone graced by a bowl perched on it - to receive the consecrated bread and *wine*. The taking of the bread and wine is discreet and rapid to avoid detection by the prison authorities. After receiving the Holy Communion, they reverently leave.

All the above observed activities carry a very profound message, especially for Dumba. These humble people endeavour to overcome their harsh condition. In defeat and disgrace, in anguish and torment they prevail. How strange is the illusion, and ultimately the hope, by which people sustain themselves. Although it is said that false hope wastes time, they never stop hoping. They change their hope by finding a better place to invest it. Dumba feels proud to be part of the indomitable human spirit. A passage from Aeschylus runs through his mind:

> Pain that cannot forget
> falls drop by drop
> upon the heart
> until in our despair
> there comes wisdom
> through the awful
> grace of God.

Dumba also realises that Archimedes was right when he said 'Give me a place to stand and I shall move the earth.'

The human mind, on its way to success, seeks to move the world, as it travels on many rocky and gravelled roads...rough unbeaten paths, by finding a place to stand, a haven, a solace, an inner peace. It is a trail blazer wrung from essentially sterner, resistant material. It survives its anguish and still build a better world, a better tomorrow, a better future.

Fourteen

PETITIONS FOR PARDON

Dumba has been in prison now for almost six months. Nothing eventful has come his way regarding his appeal at the Supreme Court. Even the date for the hearing has not been set. It seems all probable that he will remain incarcerated for the next three, four even six months.

The most frightening thing about Dumba's nightmare is that it is real. The reality could mean that the worse comes to the worst when his appeal is heard long after he has served the full unwarranted, unfair sentence. This makes a mockery of all the pious mouthings about the country having an efficient and impartial judiciary.

Dumba is not alone in this horrendous predicament. Close on three quarters of prisoners with appeals pending have them heard twelve months after the fact. Meanwhile, innocent persons would be serving unwarranted and draconian sentences.

A fellow comrade-in-agony with a worse predicament is Alex. Eighteen months ago he appeared before an utterly incompetent, semi-literate, half-baked, unfeeling and vindictive magistrate who slapped on him sixty months in the slammer, for allegedly misappropriating a sum under four thousand dollars. Poor Alex is still waiting for his case to be heard at the higher court. Proud and conceited, the experience has shattered his ego. It has made him bull simple, a whiner and a cry baby. What is most pathetic is that two thirds of the inmates are in similar untenable and cruel situations.

The worst feeling of a prisoner is the hostage effect. It is the horrible feeling that one has been forgotten, abandoned. The worst thing for the person is not the physical suffering, the incredible punishing hardships. One can learn to master the sadness, the desperation, to channel the misery. What is unbearable is the feeling of having been forgotten, having ceased to exist in the outside world, being powerless to work actively and directly to change the situation...being hopeless to do anything about it.

Then there is the punishing obstacle, *time*. How time stubbornly refuses to pass. Then the thoughts of one's cosy bed, the warmth of the spouse, the comfort of the house, the sumptuous meals. Then the waiting. Waiting is always the worst time as each man is alone with his thoughts. Truly this is rough justice! It is criminally unfair.

But luckily the human mind has the resilience to sustain the frustration, to imagine and wish that somehow a miracle changes the situation. This is the wish, the prayer, the hope that Dumba and Alex and many inmates nurse, think aloud and project.

A drowning person will clutch at a serpent. Dumba and Alex decide to do something positive about their situation: a petition to the president of the country forthwith. Thoughts have wings. Thoughts can be transmitted, received and understood by others at a distance, especially by loved ones. It seems that thought generates a mental energy which can be projected from one mind to the consciousness of another. Could it be extra sensory perception or just coincidence? Whatever it is, it seems one can influence others with one's thinking.

Outside the prison, Una and Mrs Alex, oblivious of their spouses' plan, also decide to prepare a petition to the president for the pardon and release of the husbands. The two women feel it is wise politics to use the first lady's good offices. So they address the petition to her. It reads 'Our dear First lady,

We humbly submit this petition through you in a desperate attempt to acquaint you with very serious and critical problems that have befallen our two families. These problems threaten to destroy the very existence of the two families.'

'We are presenting the following facts for your information and consideration regarding the circumstances surrounding the two families' predicament. Since the two husbands' arrest, more than twelve months ago, the two families have suffered, and continue to suffer, loss of income as the fathers who were the breadwinners, remain incarcerated and languishing in jail. They are innocent.'

'Dear First Lady, the financial and social burdens left behind after their imprisonment are colossal and make it impossible for the families to exist. The two matrimonial homes could be put on auction sale any time now. When this happens we will be left out cold, homeless and absolute squatters.'

'Accordingly, dear mother, we urge you to move in swiftly to save us, in particular the eight children who are shorn of the very basic physiological needs. As the pioneer and champion of the noble cause and campaign for child welfare and development we are convinced that you are obviously concerned. You will not allow a situation where two young families of eight children face such intolerable hardships that threaten their very survival and development.'

'As our mother we have to turn to you for help in this hour of need, in this desperate situation. Hence, we pray you to use your good offices to bring to His Excellency's attention the dire plight of our two beloved families. So we humbly urge you mother, to impress it upon his excellency, the president, to exercise his prerogative of mercy and grant our two jailed dear husbands pardon. The clemency will definitely avert the looming disaster that could leave the families stranded, homeless and destitute.'

'Our only hope, we humbly repeat our mother, our only hope and salvation is the presidential intervention in the form of clemency. We are very hopeful and confident that through you mother, his excellency, the president will accept our humble petition and grant our two very dear husbands clemency.'

Four weeks pass. The two petitioners receive a reply to their petition from the first lady. She is short, candid and to the point. She does not waste time on niceties. She says that she sympathises with the families' plight. However, there is very little she can do except to advise them to approach a lawyer who can take up their case with the appeal courts. She wishes them the best of luck in their efforts.

The two ladies study the reply, consult their husbands and resolve to persevere and press on with now a direct personal petition to the president himself. They realise that petitions through third parties fail. Their petition, direct to the president, reads

'Your Excellency, as a follow-up to our first petition to you through the First Lady, we again resubmit this petition to you as our situations and circumstances continue to deteriorate with each passing day. We are forever grateful for the concern and support shown by the first lady. Nevertheless, the dire plight of our two families leaves us no alternative but to turn to you for help.'

'Accordingly we humbly make this submission in an effort to present and highlight some of the facts and circumstances surrounding the alleged offences for which our husbands were convicted. This is a genuine attempt to furnish you with some of the many facts that the magistrates overlooked when deciding the fate of our husbands.'

'For instance, the presiding magistrates ignored the facts that: our husbands are innocent; there is no one prejudiced;

the cases were instigated by outsiders; the imprisonment meant loss of jobs, earnings and careers; there was attendant adverse publicity of the trials; there is to be restitution; they have long, loyal and illustrations services in government and the public service.'

'Your Excellency, it is fact that the situation was created, promoted and aggravated by such factors as frame ups, envy, jealousy, sheer malice and evil intentions by some work mates, subordinates a swell as other positions. They were thus, indeed victims of circumstances most of which were beyond their control.'

'It is against this background that we pray, Your Excellency, for their pardon. If granted clemency not only will our two families be relieved of a very painful situation we are in now but the nation will benefit greatly from our husbands' specialized skills and expertise which are sorely needed in boosting national development. They would be able to contribute to the national welfare through productive out put and tax contributions rather than the present position where they are forced to draw from the state coffers without putting back anything.'

'Your Excellency, we are convinced that their continued stay in jail is a kin to a gross misappropriation of skilled person-power resources at a time when they are a scarce commodity in out young fledging country ... a country that needs the efforts of every citizen.'

'We wish to emphasize, Your Excellency, that the experiences that our families have undergone have been very traumatic and the punishment extremely excessive. We have suffered considerable adverse publicity throughout the periods of trial. They have suffered loss of job, career and earnings. They, and us, continue to suffer as they remain incarcerated.'

'Furthermore, their poor health which continues to deteriorate is a cause of constant anxiety to the families. As a mater of fact, as we write, both our husbands are confined to the sick bay of the prison dispensary suffering recurring heart condition and severe asthmatic attacks, respectively.'

'Please find attached a copy of our first petition to you channeled through the first lady. We remain very

confident that Your Excellency will accept and grant our
dearest husbands clemency.'

One month passes, two, three, four, five no reply, not even
a simple acknowledgement. The president has no manners, no
feelings and no heart.
The man is deaf and blind. He sees nothing, he hears
nothing, he feels nothing. He speaks nothing. He is damn dumb.
He is still a prisoner- of his character, his ideas, his conceit, his
lack of feeling, his way of thinking, his way of behaving and his
lack of action.
This time it is his lack of action, his indifference, his
silence that is deafening. The man could preside over his own
mother's execution by watching passively. All that is needs for
evil to continue to rear its ugly head, and to prosper, is for
supposedly good people in the right positions of influence of
authority, to do nothing.

Fifteen

LESSONS FROM GEHENA

While the primary aim of a country's penal system is to reform people and make them into much more useful and creative members of society, it is very doubtful if that is being achieved. It is a hypocritical claim that borders on mythology. It is fiction.

To begin with, there is no staff trained to handle and implement a truly rehabilitation programme. Most prison staff are very poorly qualified for the job. Entry qualifications are very low with some of them barely literate. Almost all of them are lowly paid, with the lower ranks given starvation wages. Their accommodation, though free, ranges from sub standard quarters to squalid shacks. So most prison staff are not happy with their job. Like the prisoners, they are trapped and deprived of many basic things of life.

So when warders ill treat prisoners, or even misappropriate their rations, it is possible they are acting out of frustration. Some warders are known to be sadistic, insulting and persecuting. Frequently they assault, bark, grunt or scream with or without provocation. Occasionally without warning, there bursts from their lips a flood of obscenities that would make a sailor blush. These are jailers proper, partly because of their own nature but mainly because they are a product of the inhuman system.

On the credit side a tiny minority of prison officers are supportive and more helpful than is required of them. They span the whole spectrum from the lowest ranks, middle and professional officers to the higher levels. Professionally trained personnel, though still a tiny minority, like teachers, priests, nurses and artisans are warm, concerned, humane and likable. They are a cut above the rest.

In this category is a male nurse most inmates salute. Warm, affable, firm, short but tall in deeds. He is always among the first to arrive at a tragic scene. He treats prisoner and officer alike with concern for the health and welfare of the patient. It is for small but precious kindnesses, rather than spectacular events, that he is most gratefully remembered. He is never known to refuse a call for help, however unreasonable. Not uncommon are midnight calls that go with his job. The moment he steps through the door everyone begins to relax. He is direct and reassuring, banishing fears without belittling them.

Though new in the prison service he does not allow prison bureaucracy to come between him and his patient. He is clever, witty with admirable good sense of humour. In his daily contact with patients, prisoners and warders alike, he hears cries for love and attention thinly disguised as physical symptoms. He has the time to give the patient the attention that he craves for. Inmates fondly call him 'the Medic'.

Dumba helps him in the dispensary and together they make a perfect pair as they daily attend to the needs, the pains, and the anxieties, of their patients. Dumba accepts with humility the title, 'Father Doc', the young men affectionately give him. But they all take off their hats to the concern and dedication to duty of the Medic who confides to Dumba

'If we refuse attention or medication as unnecessary, the patient thinks we lack care, we lack sympathy. We can't afford to be perceived as such. It's unethical, unprofessional and insensitive.'

The lesson here is simple yet profound. We are all human beings, no matter who we are in life, who deserve love, care, and self-less service. Service to others, especially the needy, is the rent one has to pay for one's room here on earth.

Dumba also discovers that prison is a veritable store house of invaluable information on how to understand and prevent common prevalent crime. Law breakers may also be children or parents with ties to family and community. They may move in and out of the business of law breaking as their economic and social situations change. Factors that influence this decision include economic and political upheaval, economic dependency, lack of alternative job opportunities, unemployment, illiteracy and ignorance, break up of families, physical disasters - such as drought, war and migration - or sheer poverty.

For many crime is not a problem. It is a solution to grinding poverty, hunger, unemployment or powerlessness. From impoverished homes and backgrounds they are real intellectual innocents in an African country which has lost its own innocence, its own decency.

So governments, and society have to tackle these causes boldly and urgently. Both the interests of society and the requirements of common justice call for drastic reform in all these crucial and critical areas.

For the so-called criminals their world view is radical but plausible. In fact, they view the term crime as a social invention used by the powerful haves to stigmatise and victimise the powerless haves-not who try to change their harsh and cruel conditions.

Hence the rich and powerful have the weapons and power to enforce their rules, their laws and to impose their definitions of crime and deviance on the poor and less powerful. To them it is criminal that the ruling class votes itself fat salaries, allowances, perks and expensive cars when people in the slums go hungry. Consider the wife of the attorney general who has 200 pairs of shoes while in the rural areas parents cannot afford to buy their children a single pair of home made sandals.

Or the extravagant company executive who spends five thousand dollars on a lavish birthday party for his daughter, while people - his workers included - are starving a few blocks away. Have they earned or stolen the money? Who are the real criminals: those who steal for pleasure or to survive?

The same applies to ethnic groups who are prosecuted as criminals for breaking fish and game laws, for the use of marijuana yet their behaviour is neither deviant nor criminal in terms of their traditional culture. As far as they are concerned it is normal, expected and acceptable.

Then as if this is not enough, these leaders and captains of industry go on to regard the multitudes as people who cannot see the horizon...whose gaze is fixed only as far ahead as their bellies or their genitals.

And it is becoming a fashion, a custom, for the leaders to name all roads, state buildings, airports, dams, schools, hospitals and other public works after their own names, after political luminaries and mediocrities...spending huge sums of public funds in the process. In this climate of indulgence the bullies and sadists who lurk in any community take full advantage of the sanctions accorded to amass wealth, to plunder and to maim and lock up those they feel are in their way.

All these extremes leave the poor, the powerless, the trodden with no alternative but to break the powerful's laws ending up in the slammer...to languish, lick their wounds, ruminate at the same time share their experiences, and hope that the need finds the person to take them to a second liberation, true liberation...for tomorrow belongs to them.

*   *   *   *

There are also valuable lessons to learn from the operations of the crooks, the *tsotsis* themselves especially when it comes to 'crimes against property'. On the individual level there is a common, but not so obvious, factor that can successfully be tackled to prevent crime. It is the existence of a ready market for the law breakers' services. Through either a deliberate or inadvertent connivance the individual collaborates as source or market for their services. Dumba is struck with this obvious fact as he talks to the inmates. His talk with them is so revealing and strange yet so true.

Most of the *tsotsis* say that they study their victims before they get down to work. They do some in-depth research on behaviour, habits, weaknesses and strengths.

The young mugger says he picked his victims by looking for isolated people who shuffled along, heads down, eyes averted, and who seemed frightened when they saw him. He would not try anything with a person who looked right into his eyes, who examined him up and down from head to toe as if s/he were sizing him up. He read body language that predicted a successful attack.

The serious burglar does his home work thoroughly not only noting times the victim leaves and returns home but tries to enlist the help of an insider such as a worker or casual relation. In fact a daring young man here boasts of successfully burgling a post office almost single handed with the help of one very ordinary post office worker. He and the post office sweeper took four months planning, patiently cutting the keys to the doors and safe. They netted twenty seven thousand dollars, in one sweep, at the end of the day.

Car 'takers' also employ an elaborate net work of spying and tracking down their victims. They usually work in two groups with a get away car ready. Using sophisticated master keys and devices they quickly enter the car, render the alarm safe or break the anti theft-device...start or push the car and off they go followed, at a safe distance, by the get away car. They tell Dumba that the most effective anti-theft device is to either leave a grown up person in the car or to remove, and take with you, the distributor rotor arm. That is how they themselves safe guard their own vehicles from 'takers'. Dogs and young children are not effective.

110

All the *tsotsis* are in total agreement that they thrive on the most common of human weaknesses. These are sheer carelessness, ignorance and lack of commonsense. They say that commonsense is not that common. In fact it is a very special sense. People never learn. To illustrate this they tell this joke. A drunk was walking down the street with both ears blistered, and he met a friend who asked what happened. The drunk explained:

'My wife left her hot pressing iron next to the phone when she left the room to answer to the urgent call of nature. The phone rang and I picked up the iron by mistake.'

'But what about the other ear?' asked the friend. He replied

'The fool called back!'

So by heeding these warnings people can keep the crooks, snatchers and pick-pockets not only at bay but out of pocket. This is the way to beat the crime industry. Anyone can become a victim, they tell Dumba. Bus and cinema queues, busy street corners, large shopping centres, crowded places, isolated corners; crowded banking halls are choice hunting grounds for those in the crime industry.

They concentrate on the central city areas and wealthy suburbs at week ends. They have the smell for money. They know when pay day has arrived, and are particularly busy during seasonal shopping rushes such as at bonus time, Christmas and Easter which bring crowds with money to spend. Laden with parcels, the unwary shopper, or traveller presents an easy target.

They may operate alone but usually they work with a gang. They are rarely amateurs. More often they are hard-boiled fellows, as wily as they are tough. They are quick fingered and quick footed. Well dressed people, who look as though they may have a lot of money, are preferred victims. A 'bumper' will jostle the victim, barge into her and deftly remove her purse. Or he may be direct in his attack, rushing at her and tearing her bag away or slitting its straps with a razor-sharp knife if it is loosely slung. Those in the profession call this style 'the cracking whip', partly because the bag is made of leather and also the cracking scream and shouts of the victim realising too late that the bag is gone.

A 'carrier' is ready to take the bag from the snatcher if he is caught. This ordinary looking accomplice goes unnoticed in a crowd, and only comes forward if he is needed. Sometimes the two will pass the bag from one to the other to confuse pursuers. Or they swop jackets to avoid detection. There may be a third member, a decoy, who runs off without the bag, effectively drawing attention away from the others. The decoy is fast and sure footed...faster than the sprinting cheetah.

The elite and professional employ the 'fork' movement. It is a technique in which they use the first and middle fingers of their long, sensitive hands, as though they were a pair of scissors, to surreptitiously fish a purse out of a handbag or inner pocket. They call it 'nice and clean' since the victim is blissfully unaware of what is happening. They often distract a victim's attention by shouting at a partner ahead or stepping in front of her.

To illustrate their skills to Dumba they approach a rather sleepy warder nearby. They first take off his belt, then fish out his underpants, then his sock...all done without awakening him. They, however, leave the 'loot' neatly arranged before the warder's feet.

A few use cruder methods as they carry knives to threaten victims who resist. They are nicked-named the 'Savages', Tanga men'. The sight of a cut-throat knife is usually enough to persuade a reluctant victim to give in. They are tough as forged steel and sharp as a new razor blade. This group, as its members grow old and less agile, tends to specialise in breaking into cars in search of cash and valuables.

However, the professionals perfect their skills and methods of operations. A favourite ploy is for them to approach a motorist when s/he stops at a traffic light. They tell the targeted victim that the rear tyre is flat. When the victim climbs out to investigate, stealing valuables, or even the car itself is easy.

A variation to this ruse is to walk up to a woman in her car in the park. Suddenly, he leans through the open window and kiss her. By the time she has recovered from the shock he would have disappeared with her bag or valuables. They invent so many ruses that one should be wary of even attending to 'first aid cases that appear to need attention'.

Even offers of help from strangers who look harmless, like uniformed members of religious sects, should be regarded with suspicion since they are fraught with danger. Saints, genuine Samaritans are in very short supply these days...even those in religious clothing. They are a rare species in these troubled times.

Carrying large sums of money in a bag is inviting trouble. The *tsotsis* often make a careful study of such people's movements. Money smells. It has an inviting odour that attracts even the most innocent. Worse, it attracts more those with ugly intentions. They smell money just as flies detect smell from a long distance. So they are wide awake to such ruses as carrying money in innocent looking shopping bags or shoe boxes.

So it is wise to carry just enough money one needs. If it is unavoidable to carry large sums, the money should be divided in several pockets or purses. Inside zipped pockets are safer. This is how the *tsotsis* also keep their money safe from other predators, they tell Dumba. A purse held in the mouth, or carried by a child, or in a basket or trolley is an open invitation to a snatcher. Never open a full purse in the presence of bystanders or leave it on the counter when making purchases.

When driving with the window open, it is safer to place your bag under your seat or in the locked boot. The *tsotsis* also advise Dumba to always keep alert in crowded places, never to doze...and to move instantly if jostled.

Finally, they advise Dumba that alertness and knowledge of the crooks' techniques and possible ploys are the best means of assuring he will not become a victim. Above all, they tell him, believe no one, trust nobody and be suspicious of every one's moves and motives...and even the movement of your own shadow. Human beings are born of faults and are motivated by self interest. They are not motivated by charitable intentions. No human being is charitable, though they would swear to God that they are. A rather strange tricky world to live in, Dumba reflects.

Sixteen

MIXED FORTUNES

Dumba carefully but impatiently flips through the previous week's newspapers. He mutters and swears under his moustache about the savage cuts and senseless censorship of the papers by the prison authorities. Besides the stale news, in fact now history, the mutilated paper is delicate, fragile and distorted. He does not find anything important. He is about to push the papers away.

Suddenly, his eye's attention is caught by an article in the family notices column. He cannot believe his eyes. He seems to be dreaming. He pinches himself. He is wide awake. There, under *death* notices is the name of a very dear, close personal friend Fari Dan. Dumba chilled, shocked and grief stricken tries to hold back tears. He could hear his heart throbbing and thumbing in his ears. He almost chokes with tears as he reads the sombre, sad and mournful messages.

Dan's wife thanks him for twenty four good years, though he has gone without saying good bye. She promises him that she will look after the children. She sombrely asks the Lord to rest her dear husband in peace till they are joined together again.

The next message is from Dan's nephew who acknowledges that Dan was more of a friend to him than a 'father'. Death had snatched him away so suddenly. Though he has been relieved of all the pain he suffered for the little time he was allowed to live after the accident, he has left a vacuum in their lives, no other person can ever fill. The nephew wonders aloud who is going to advise them ? All that kindness, thoughtfulness, smile, humour is no more. He ends his message by extending sympathy to aunt and the rest of the family. Dumba is to learn much later that the nephew was driving Dan in his car when the fatal car collision took place. The nephew escaped with minor scratches to the arm and leg.

The next message is the most touching, the most moving. It comes from Dan's five children. The blow, the loss, is too much for them. One could feel it from the tone of the message. They advise

'those who still have their fathers to love them while you can. You do not know what it is like to lead life without one'.

They collectively ask dear God, if there are roses in heaven, to please pick the best bunch for him. They plead with God to keep him safely till they meet again. They end by thanking their dad for all the love and for everything else that came with it. They pray him to rest in peace.

Another message is from Dan's sister and her children:

'In dreams we see your face;
memories and time cannot erase.

We will love and miss you for the
rest of our lives. Fly free: God is your co-pilot. Your loving sister Jannie and children.'

Yet another requiem comes from his colleagues at work. They were shocked and saddened to learn of the death of a most valuable member. His passing away creates a vacancy that will be hard to fill. He did far more than the normal person's share of work. Whenever there was a job to do, he did it...a helping hand needed, he provided it. They ask a rhetorical but pertinent question

'Dear God, why do you always only take the best ? Please tell us.'

They end by bidding Dan farewell though he did not say good bye. He will be badly .missed by all who knew him. He was difficult to hate. They ask him to rest in peace, a dear friend and colleague.

Dumba's mind floats and drifts to the times when he and Fari had worked and stayed together. All the memories of their life together rise in a flood into his throat. They were so close that they had called one another 'my son'. No one could make out who was the 'father'.

Dumba remembers him as a trusted friend with a keen sense of humour and an infectious grin. A fountain of humour and funny stories he had people always in stitches with laughter. He invariably wore a smile or had one lurking, and was always looking for a way to let it out. He was excellent company.

He had a hundred of stories, both true and apocryphal, with which to entertain and amuse friends and colleagues. As a teacher and lecturer Fari once had to illustrate The Parable of the Good Samaritan. Fari Dan's version to his students was typical.

He told his very attentive students a story about a lady called Irene. Irene was moving with the crowd on a busy city street when a young man in front of her was stopped by an attractive woman. The woman greeted him and said something. As Irene tried to negotiate her way and manoeuvre around them, he grabbed Irene's arm and said to the woman

'And I would like you to meet my fiancée".'

'It's so nice to meet you,' the woman said eagerly. Well what the heck. Irene thought.

'It's nice to meet you too,' Irene replied.

'When is the wedding ?' The woman asked

'Next month,' the man answered

'A small thing, really,' Irene said

'If you can call four hundred people small,' he chimed.

The three of them chatted gaily, said their good byes, and the woman went off. The young man grasped Irene's hand

'Thank you,' he said fervently. 'That was my ex-girl friend.'

That was Dan, the teacher, the administrator, the unforgettable character, a legendary who loved and adored people, children, music, life and humour. A grateful student who undoubtedly worshipped him once referred to him as 'our father who art at 46 Smuts Road.' With a unique blend of informality, kindness and concern he captivated all who met him. Dan's weaknesses were few: bend-over-backward tolerance, modesty, kindness, a love of his beer and cigarette.

To Dumba he was a cheerful friend, who like the sunny day spread brightness all round. He painfully wishes his friend were here, for in times like these, when cheerfulness seems to be a rare commodity, you need a friend like Dan to come to the rescue. Dumba is sure that Dan is telling amusing stories and jokes all the way to the pearly gates. He feels he can hear his hearty, wholesome laughter in paradise. Dumba, on his part though he dares not hope to enter the city of God, hears himself say, angel Gabriel move over, here comes Dan!

The immortal words of the Preacher keep ringing in Dumba's ears uplifting him to new heights

'Death is swallowed

up in victory. O death

where is thy victory ? O

death where is thy sting ?'

Dumba is jerked out of the sad stupor by a tap on the shoulder from an inmate. He hands him a letter that, as usual, has been censored. Dumba could tell by the neat, beautiful handwriting that it is from his eldest child.

Dumba's children have been the greatest joys of his life, his wife aside of course. They have grown up in a very positive atmosphere for children. Dumba and wife relish their children. They watch their openness, and the originality and joy they bring to everything they do, and bring the couple back on balance.

And here is this child, this bright incandescent one, bringing colour to a dreary placed called prison. The news is a balm to his tangled emotions, tormented soul and troubled spirit. It nourishes the mind.

The letter salutes in typical style.

'Hello dad ! This is me here saying how are you ? I'm sure and I trust that you're very well. We're all doing very well here and Cha is studying very diligently for the June exams. I know the fellow will do wonders. As you must already know, our O'level results are out. I went to collect them today. I'm glad to say that I got 4 As, 4 Bs and 2 Cs. but dad I'm very disappointed with my French results. Imagine I got a bloody E ! Really, dad, something went wrong somewhere because French to me looked easy. I would have thought that may be the school could trace my papers to have them remarked. I don't know what you suggest but really I'm convinced that something went wrong somewhere. It really doesn't sound and look like me at all.'

This afternoon we met uncle and aunt and they gave me ten dollars for what they both called a brilliant performance. With the ten dollars I bought for myself a school tie which cost me nine dollars eighty, leaving me with twenty cents change. Really it's absurd how expensive things are nowadays. What an expensive world dad ?'

'But honestly dad, I was disappointed with English literature which was failed badly at school. Extended science was worse. Just for interest sake, in my class, the pupils did very well. The highest had 8 As and 1 B. The second highest had 7 As and a C. That's what I call brilliant performance. Over all in my class, every one passed with the exception of one poor boy.'

'Forgive me, dad, for talking too much. Now it's decision time. I intend to go for A' level of course and do English, mathematics, biology and chemistry. What do you think? Is that a wise decision? I know that may be you might say why not take geography. But to me geography is war. As for maths, as you know I enjoy it very much. So I know I'll do well.'

'Change of subject dad. Here is an old Chinese saying which goes like this: *Listen to a person who has paid for wisdom in the heavy coin of experience. So it pays to stoop to conquer.* Yet another one says: *He who runs away lives to fight again. Don't mistake him/her for a coward.* The Nubians say: *The two most powerful warriors are patience, and resilience..courage is a virtue in the midst of misfortune.* And here is the last saying from Eric Hoffer, in The Passionate State Of Mind: *Our credulity is greatest concerning the things we know least about. And since we know least about ourselves, we are ready to believe all that is said about us. Hence the mysterious power of both flattery and calumny.* I don't know if you'll be able to make head or tail of these seemingly unrelated sayings so I'll explain it all with another quotation from Peter MacArthur: *One should never spoil a good theory by explaining it!'*

'Oh dad let's leave the world of riddles and give you some news about my friends. My friend in USA, Jennifer from Redondo Beach in California, wrote to me some time ago. She is great. She sent me some wonderful things - a pure silver necklace with a pearl fitted in the centre, a magic tree which grows into a beautiful tree in just 15 minutes. That I've saved till you come home. And I know that you will be coming very soon. We want you to join in the fun of watching it grow. She also sent me a cushion full of roses that have a super smell. That, my friend said, I was to keep in my clothes so that they have a nice refreshing smell.'

'My other friend from New Zealand, Ngatai in Auckland did send me a *friendly band.* And then my other friend Samir, you remember that one you used to joke about saying he lives behind someone else's bungalow, has finished his studies in India. He is now studying medicine at the University of Netherlands or something like that. His father has sent me a Christmas card. He is the one who has informed me of Samir's new address. Really I was honoured. It was kind and nice of him.'

'Yet another international friend of mine has written from Papua New Guinea. She is Wanganui. She's 18. She drinks and smokes a little. She lives with her sister and two kids. She wants to be a nurse for the old. Wanganui strongly believes that the aged are the only two legged endangered species on earth. So they need care and attention. She sent me this poem, what she calls an Ode To Old Mother:

> *When did you last go home to mother ?*
> *Courageous, proud.*
> *Never saying anything.*
> *Sitting. Waiting.*

Growing old.
Thinking of a world gone by.
Of children
Playing in the garden.
Caring, coping,
Encouraging, loving
always understanding.
Until now.
When a day in a life time,
And just one friendly face
Is golden sunshine.
You will come, won't you?

Care for the aged,
They cared for you.'

'My other pen friend is Douane of Australia. She is at a girls' college and wants to be a kangaroo cum dairy farmer in future. Really that's beyond my own imagination. For my part if I decide to get involved in the farming business then the last I could do is to become a kangaroo farmer. It's better to be a vet. My plans in future are, as you know, to go to university of course and take up either medicine or pharmacy. Or probably quantity surveying. That's my goal in life. U-m-m I think that about wraps up everything for now.'

'Good gracious dad, I had forgotten to tell you about the rest of the family. They would roast me if I fail to convey news about them. Ti is doing quite well in the first grade with a Ms San. Fu is just great. Ga is fantastic. As for Cha that one is the star. Ro is naughtier than ever. As for me I intend to work very hard. We promise you we'll do wonders. There is no doubt about that. We're all very well. Grandma and granddad are all right. Occasionally grandma whizzes and sneezes but expectorates. Granddad coughs and hunts noisily for breath but recovers.'

'From all of us out here we say: Just hang on in there. It's only a matter of time. That's all. We all love you dad. Cheers!'

Half an hour later Dumba is startled to attention by noise and actions coming towards him. It is the kind of noise that calls attention to itself. A rather clumsy, huge young man called Buster ambles, swinging his big dish-shaped head. Suddenly he leaps and spins in the air as if stung by a bee, careening and prancing. He is joined in the unrehearsed acrobatics by more than half a dozen inmates. *Leap for joy. Dance for joy,* they shout.

Before Dumba could inquire about the reason for the impromptu celebration cum antics they mob him with the huge one hugging him. It is a bear hug, a vice grip that empties Dumba's lungs of air. Buster measures nearly two metres and looks like the kind of fellow who eats rusty cycle chains for breakfast. Amid gasps for air Dumba learns that his strange fans have passed their O' level examinations.

Somehow Dumba manages to free himself from the crushing crowd. The fellows feel themselves like balloons filling with the helium of success. For the first time in the history of the prison school 80% of them have passed their O' level English examinations. Hardly a single person had passed it before. Most of them had attempted the examination four or five times but in vain. So naturally they attribute their brilliant performance and incredible success to Dumba, the teacher, and to no one else.

The young men see brilliant careers ahead of them when they leave prison. Without a full O' level certificate there is no hope of a well paid job, or of even getting a job. In the intoxicated state they are in now they brim over with self-congratulation. They rub their hands, stroke themselves, and lie on the ground drunk on praise and self-satisfaction. They sing, dance, shout, whistle and jive for joy. They shower Dumba with accolades as they call him the 'saviour of the suffering and ignorant'.

Dumba remains humble as he relates their success to hard work, zeal, single-mindedness of purpose on their part. He tells them that learning is one of the greatest earthly joys, the one that should accompany them through their life's journey in this world.

As the Chinese say, *a great and rewarding journey of a thousand kilometres starts with a single step.* So what they get from teachers and schools is but one of the many steps on the life-long journey of learning, living, discovery, and rediscovering themselves, and the environment. So it is just the beginning of the exciting, challenging, and sometimes daunting, voyage of discovery. To those who take and stand up to the challenges the rewards are handsome and immeasurably satisfying.

Seventeen

HOME COMING

It all starts with the incredible, startling news of drastic changes in fortunes and circumstances. Then the impossible happens. A miracle, an impossibility.

Even with the best of moments in life one cannot help feeling having a picnic under Vesuvius. That kind of a journey in life comes to every one, chief Makope included. The ever watchful eyes of fate make sure the cruel and evil-doers are properly punished. So fate is to deal Makope a cruel blow. Those with a sharper instinct for survival read the omens and escape from evil. They see the sword coming and they sound the drum. But at times tragedy haunts the cruel and unfortunate as a lesson to those who decide to follow the path of evil.

The news comes unexpectedly. Makope is dropped from the cabinet. He is not even availed of the usual formality of being warned in advance. He has to be told by ordinary people who have just listened to the radio broadcast. Yes the local chief is fired, is jobless, desperate, derobed. The mighty fall. How are the mighty fallen. Luck uncharacteristically changes sides.

Fiction writers would blush at inventing the dramas that, at times, take place in this world. From a Mercedes Benz to hitching a lift. From a fat salary to selling eggs in a small basket...and rotten tomatoes for a living. All in a space of two months. Incredible! The gods and fate can punish. At times it seems that God and fate take a direct hand in people's affairs.

This man who, just yesterday, was a powerful man is now a walking contradiction. Quiet, soft spoken but cursed with a puerile grudge, a perpetual pout that denies others and him of joy. A man who, like the proverbial elephant, never forgets and never forgives. He who craved to be feared the way other people need to be liked. It all sadly adds up to a torn and complex character, boiling with talents of hate, cruelty and emotions. Some people, and animals, overcome ugliness with charming personalities. Not this devil hated and loathed even by his own offspring.

The worst part of his character is that he is a killer. He has the instinct of the leopard who kills for the taste of blood and the simple joy of it. He has the venomous glare. Yes, he is more of the African black mamba, the most dreaded of all Africa's snakes. Its venom, and speed in striking are the most lethal. Unlike its counterpart, the rattle snake it strikes without warning. It can inflict death on a fully grown person in four minutes. Its strike is so swift as to cheat the eye.

But faced with Dumba's bravery and resilience the mamba has its match in the African honey badger. The badger has a loose but thick tough skin that can defy the bite of a mastiff, or the vicious fangs of the leopard. It is endowed with a massive flattened skull from which the heaviest club bounces off harmlessly. More than that, it has the heart of a lion, the courage of a provoked, irate bear. It is said that it possesses an instinct for the groin as it rushes in to rip the balls out of any man, male animal or lion, who provoke it.

Makope, the mamba, has finally been defanged...castrated by Dumba, the badger, though this is done vicariously. Makope is now the bully caught in his own snare. Yes true to form, there has come to him that bitterest moment in the life of an official, the moment when his upward career comes to a full stop. This full stop arrived and every one perceived it.

The cruel man, the monster, has reached his destined limits, in a very short space of time. His official race is run. Power, sweet delicious power, has run out. The mouth that was full of honey is now over-flowing with bile. The bed of thorns he has been busy making commands him to lie on it. These are now the thorns of his position.

Now he has been humbled. He has fallen flat on his face after futile attempts to climb the ladder of success from the top. All that is left of him is a hollow shell whose voice has a sound of a tired piece of sand paper calling o its mate. Life can be generous, but when abused it can be cruel as well.

Hostility born of fear and malice is universally the product of ignorance and lack of foresight. Hatred and antagonism can blind one totally. How can one make the blind man see? Malice like the curse, comes home to roost. Apostles, of doom and destruction, like those of dictatorship, have unpleasant endings.

What is left are memories...small sores that refuse to heal. It is sad but curious to see chief Makope transform into *povo* Makope overnight, feeling hollow, as if his working parts are somewhere else and only his clothes and skin there with him.

With Makope over, gone and done with, former friends waste no tears on their departed comrade. His woman bed-fellows like Zariri take their services to new powerful masters with renewed vigour. There is nothing about them that shows contrition from an ancient evil that is as enthralling as sin itself. She goes into it with the sexual appetite that she has known many a man. She has experienced ever}[7] possible variation of style, rhythm, position, size, shape and colour...seeking always an elusive fulfillment which seems to dance for ever beyond her grasp.

With the men she chooses, no further effort would be required from her...the men's genius would provide the means and the moment, and it is part of the excitement. All the sensual pleasures beckons her irresistibly, like a fly to milk.

But for poor Makope all this thought is bitter. His friends have now deserted him. In this they show a rather ugly, beastly trait, but they are realists. Power - like fame, money or sex - lasts the span of dew. False friends are like our shadows, keeping close to us while we walk in the sunshine, but leaving us the instant we cross into the shade. With friends like these who needs enemies. Chief Makope's praise-singers have vanished. People want winners not losers. As said before, fame is like dew. It is very transient. Though glistening and impressive in the early morning it does not last for a tiny fraction of the day.

Poetic justice is slow but sure. What has happened to the sting of the man who boasted: *I am the master of destruction, the father of disaster. I make and destroy kings. I am terror itself. Dumha I will destroy you!* All that is left of him is the venom and phlegm carried in his vial as he goes on meaningless sex rampages like a man who has just discovered sex rather very late...rather too late in the evening of his life. He is a sure *aids* candidate. Any way who cares. His death would be good riddance of bad rubbish.

While now *povo* Makope licks his wounds in shame Dumba recovers and, like the rising sun shines even brighter. Sometimes, accidents and misfortunes, even formless things come to shape the pattern of our lives. One thing is certain: the star we were born under will determine our fate and our future. Time is the best historian, the fairest judge, and the most accurate fore-teller. Such a combination of science, fiction and fate is impossible to beat.

Dumba's luck and miracles are still operating. Good luck and fate take a direct hand in his affairs. The miracles are holding. For what Dumba and family have been craving for happens.

After a very long and painful wait in jail the Supreme Court finds Dumba innocent and acquits him. lie is vindicated. The law, though, is not an exact science nor is it an accurate art. It is rational knowledge subject to speculation, inference and conjecture bordering on guess work. At best it Now he has been humbled. He has fallen flat on his face after futile attempts to climb the ladder of success from the top. All that is left of him is a hollow shell whose voice has a sound of a tired piece of sand paper calling to its mate. Life can be generous, but when abused it can be cruel as well.

Hostility born of fear and malice is universally the product of ignorance and lack of foresight. Hatred and antagonism can blind one totally. How can one make the blind man see ? Malice like the curse, comes home to roost. Apostles, of doom and destruction, like those of dictatorship, have unpleasant endings.

What is left are memories...small sores that refuse to heal. It is sad but curious to see chief Makope transform into *povo* Makope overnight, feeling hollow, as if his working parts are somewhere else and only his clothes and skin there with him.

With Makope over, gone and done with, former friends waste no tears on their departed comrade. His woman bed-fellows like Zariri take their services to new powerful masters with renewed vigour. There is nothing about them that shows contrition from an ancient evil that is as enthralling as sin itself. She goes into it with the sexual appetite that she has known many a man. She has experienced every possible variation of style, rhythm, position, size, shape and colour...seeking always an elusive fulfillment which seems to dance for ever beyond her grasp.

With the men she chooses, no further effort would be required from her...the men's genius would provide the means and the moment, and it is part of the excitement. All the sensual pleasures beckons her irresistibly, like a fly to milk.

But for poor Makope all this thought is bitter. His friends have now deserted him. In this they show a rather ugly, beastly trait, but they are realists. Power - like fame, money or sex - lasts the span of dew. False friends are like our shadows, keeping close to us while we walk in the sunshine, but leaving us the instant we cross into the shade. With friends like these who needs enemies. Chief Makope's praise-singers have vanished. People want winners not losers. As said before, fame is like dew. It is very transient. Though glistening and impressive in the early morning it does not last for a tiny fraction of the day.

Poetic justice is slow but sure. What has happened to the sting of the man who boasted: / *am the master of destruction, the father of disaster. I make and destroy kings. I am terror itself. Dumba I will destroy you* ! All that is left of him is the venom and phlegm carried in his vial as he goes on meaningless sex rampages like a man who has just discovered sex rather very late...rather too late in the evening of his life. He is a sure *aids* candidate. Any way who cares. His death would be good riddance of bad rubbish.

While now *povo* Makope licks his wounds in shame Dumba recovers and, like the rising sun shines even brighter. Sometimes, accidents and misfortunes, even formless things come to shape the pattern of our lives. One thing is certain: the star we were born under will determine our fate and our future. Time is both the best historian, the fairest judge, and the most accurate fore-teller. Such a combination of science, fiction and fate is impossible to beat.

Dumba's luck and miracles are still operating. Good luck and fate take a direct hand in his affairs. The miracles are holding. For what Dumba and family have been craving for happens.

After a very long and painful wait in jail the Supreme Court finds Dumba innocent and acquits him. He is vindicated. The law, though, is not an exact science nor is it an accurate art. It is rational knowledge subject to speculation, inference and conjecture bordering on guess work. At best it is guesstimate. That is why we have plenty of injustice. That is why we have appeal courts like the supreme court.

Granted, while the supreme court has the last word it does not necessarily follow that it is right. Most of the time it, like its counterpart the magistrate court, blunders. This time around it is right.

But is it fair...is it just that an innocent person stays behind bars for twelve months? What kind of justice is this? What creatures administer such a cruel system? Why are they so desensitised that they have no feelings for fellow human beings? Were they born of mothers and fathers we know? Were they sired by vampires and zombies? As far as we know they are not human. They are at best manimals. Somewhere half way between human and beast. They are the epitome of the snout of the beast coming out full blast to create havoc.

It is very strange that there are so many things we take for granted: the love and care of the loved one, of parents, of children, of friends and colleagues. The cosy bed, the warmth of the spouse, the comfort of the house, the sumptuous meals...all are great and wonderful. It is strange but true that you cannot miss what you have not experienced. To Dumba home, sweet home, entices him, calls him, usurps him, absorbs him. He goes to it in spite of himself, as the honey-bird goes to the source of honey.

Ever since Dumba has been told of his innocence and acquittal he has not relaxed. At times it is better not to know about certain things, and get a surprise. For you cannot miss what you do not know.

There is also the unnerving, nagging feeling that in Africa a person can be filled with hope at dawn and sick with despair by noon. You never know what may be coming next. So sleep refuses to come to him like a recalcitrant child called to go on an errand. Sleep becomes very slippery and elusive. The panic and helplessness seem to have taken deep root in the soul and incubate there, growing into a nameless fear that now follows him around.

Waiting is always the worst time. This is torture by boredom. Time passes in a painfully slow motion. Una, children and family wait, listen and anticipate with bated breath.

And yes, the awaited time arrives. Una rushes towards him, her hips swaying as though she is dancing to a distant music but with her head and shoulders not moving. She embraces him, wraps him, envelopes him in her arms. For a moment she is lost for words. She is thrilled with a delicious shock. All she says is

'Oh my love, my angel, my life, my happiness, my treasure you have come. Thank God and the spirits of our ancestors we have survived human intrigues, deceptions, cruelty and corruption. We have fought off the beast of despair. Is it true, is it real we're together again?'

What more can a faithful woman, wife, who scrimped and saved to make all ends meet, who has made untold sacrifices, say. She could do anything for him. They have dared so much, seen so much, shared so much. It is more than friendship, more than love...a bond that no deed, no passage of time can sever.

They are filled with a sense of destiny, the knowledge that they will help change the world. For life is serving a hard, tough, unrelenting apprenticeship. They have learnt the hard lesson that: there is nobody they can rely upon but themselves, there is no way to survive but through their own strength and determination. So they have to go on being strong and hard beyond this life, even beyond life after life.

They realise that no matter what, they still have each other. They lock together breathing each other's breath, sweet and refreshing as ever.. This is it again the fine noon of their love. The taste of freedom, of love, is indescribably delicious. The love they have is strengthened beyond measure. Because those months were denied them, every moment they now share is more precious. The matchless love they have for each other blends intricately with the big three: faith, resilience and hope - but love being the greatest.

The children and friends are less philosophical and sentimental. They hug Dumba and throw an instant celebration. Suddenly a man near Dumba pulls his cap over his eyes and begins to sing a happy African ballad. The old man next to him takes his hand to give him strength to sing. Then it is taken up immediately by all the other people in the welcoming group. The lovely chorus of African voices rising and sinking...and weaving the intricate tapestry of sound and music thrills the ear and raises the goose flesh on the skins of the listeners.

As if at an invisible signal the song and beat shift and change to a faster pace. The group leaps to life. It is like a theatre of fun. A young woman's voice rises into the air, singing the words of an ancient yet very relevant song. Tongues twirl high pitched screams. Voices chant. Feet prance like cats' paws that have stepped onto red hot hearth-stones by mistake. They leap and spin in the air shouting Dumba's praises and those of his family...their blood coming to the boil, their mesmeric influence spreads like the spell of a cobra's swaying dance before a bird trying to break the fatal hypnotism.

Yet again the song changes to a moving deep tune intended to celebrate the present happy occasion. The song extols the virtues of courage, strength and determination in the face of misfortune. Dumba, the song acknowledges, has always been resilient, with extraordinary recuperative powers. It is a lively, bracing tune, and it is sung by people who react emotionally to its message. A message of hope, courage, indomitable spirit against all odds. A celebration of the successful response to the call to rise and walk.

And, the singing, the very voice of Africa is melodious, beautiful as their voices rise and fall to the eternal rhythm of Africa. It is an expression of such pride and unutterable joy that Dumba feels his throat close up and tears sting his eye-lids. His heart pumps and thrills to the rhythms and pulse of this lovely continent. The singing is lusty and clear, with many voices in harmony, but it has, like most African tunes, an undertone of frustration and melancholy in it. It is so appropriate, so absolutely close to its physical and human setting.

And my goodness, the sound of the pulsating drum. If any one wants to know the African heart one should listen to its drum. In the flickering light, the men and women, their faces absorbed in an expression beyond knowing enter the trance-like stage as they dance to the haunting sound of the taut drum. The blood begins to rise, to sing, boil and thunder in the ears...the drum becomes their pulse.

The caress of the sun, and its warmth revive them as they sing and dance with joy. Watching the happy folk sing and dance in the palm of infinity...sitting there in the dying sun, listening to the mystic sounds of the African dusk, the gentle muted orchestra of insect, bird, animal and human, are wonderful to the ear and soul.

Dumba looks from eye to eye, and suddenly the stars seem within reach. All this stirs Dumba's warmest emotions. His own feet begin to tap. He feels envious of this health and mirthfulness, and yearns to take part in this expression of joy at being alive. Happiness and joy fill the space of sadness and misery. He has a feeling of special pride and gratitude.

Out of darkness he has been cast into light, out of a stench into a flagrant garden, out of death into life. To be free is wonderful. It is being born again. Here comes the truly happy ending and the beginning of an exciting life ahead. Dumba is now as free as unpolluted air, as free as the singing African bird It is a heart warming reunion.

Strangely, at this moment he realises that he is truly home. Here, where he left with sadness and invisible tears, he has returned with joy and a message of everlasting peace amid overflowing joy. This is indeed a celebration of life and happiness. This is his spot, and centre, of happiness. *Home.* It is where one's best friends are and live. Nothing can ever take its place. No one can ever take their place. This is it: a real home coming. It is the real feeling, the real thing!

So all bad, ugly and uncomfortable things, as with all good, sweet and comfortable things, must finally come to an end. Sorrow and joy, despair and hope, tenderness and triumph follow one another like the incoherent thoughts of a lunatic. And they vanish,

ike the emotions of a lunatic, as suddenly as they have appeared.
But all this fits somehow into the scheme of things. life is strange
out fascinating.

After travelling the smooth and rocky road of life - fun,
happiness; then enter unhappiness, tears, super aching pain - now
back to relief and sheer joy. Indeed there is something about life that
s incomplete, unfinished yet exciting. This is what challenges the
human life, what charges its batteries, what prods it to go on
with the business of living. That is why one should never take life
too seriously. And the will to win against all odds is the single most
important asset in the gruelling game of life.

At this point Dumba hears himself drawing lessons and
inspiration from the wisened whispering of the veteran author of the
Desiderata:

Go placidly amid the noise and haste, and
remember what peace there may be in silence.
As far as possible without surrender be on
good terms with all persons. Speak your truth
quietly and clearly;
and listen to others,
even the dull and ignorant;
they too have their story.

Avoid loud and aggressive persons; they are
vexations to the spirit. If you compare yourself
with others, you may become vain and bitter, f
or there will be greater and lesser
persons than yourself.
Enjoy your achievements
as well as your plans.

Keep interested in your own career,
however humble;
It is a real possession in the changing
fortunes of time.

Exercise caution in your business affairs;
for the world is full of trickery. But let
this not blind you to what
virtue there is;

Many persons strive for high ideals; and
everywhere life is full of heroism.

Be yourself,
Especially, do not feign affection.
Neither be cynical about love;
for in the face of all aridity and
disenchantment it is perennial as the grass..
Take kindly the counsel of the years, gracefully surrendering the
things of youth.
Nurture strength of spirit to shield you
in sudden misfortune.

But do not distress yourself with
imaginings.
Many fears are bom of fatigue and
loneliness.
Beyond a wholesome discipline,
be gentle with yourself.
You are a child of the universe,
no less than the trees and the stars;
you have a right to be here.
And whether or not it is clear to you,
no doubt the universe is unfolding
as it should.

Therefore be at peace with Nature,
whatever you conceive it to be,
and whatever your labours and
aspirations, in the noisy confusion of life
keep peace with your soul.

With all its sham,
drudgery and broken dreams, it is still a
beautiful world. Take care.
Strive to be happy, to excel and to win.

www.ingramcontent.com/pod-product-compliance
Lightning Source LLC
Chambersburg PA
CBHW032252070726

47590CB00016B/2564